I0721324

KING'S PROMISE

A DARK MAFIA ROMANCE

VOLKOV BRATVA

ZOE BETH GELLER

KINKY INK PUBLISHING, LLC

Copyright © 2022 Zoe Beth Geller
Kinky Ink Publishing, LLC.
All rights reserved.
Cover Design Shephard Designs

No part of this book may be reproduced or transmitted in any form or by any means, electronic or mechanical, including photocopying, recording, or by any information storage and retrieval system without the written permission of the author, except for the use of brief quotations in reviews.

This steamy romance is a work of fiction. Names, characters, places, and incidents are either products of the author's imagination or are used fictitiously. Any resemblance to actual persons, living or dead, events, or locales is entirely coincidental. The author acknowledges the trademarked status and trademark owners of various products referenced in this work of fiction, which have been used without their permission. The publication/use of these trademarks is not authorized nor sponsored by the trademark owners. This e-book is licensed for your personal use only.

Trigger warnings: kidnapping, deaths, betrayal, withholding emotion, possessive, dominant male

INTRODUCTION

In a world governed by power and vicious allegiances, Nikolay, the reluctant heir to Russia's mafia throne, finds himself plunged into a life fraught with danger and clandestine traditions. Following the death of his formidable father, the now-don, he's bound by a time-honored arranged marriage meant to merge the realms of two dominant families.

As the frost of the Russian underworld nips at his heels, Nikolay journeys to the heart of London, a city where secrets from the shadows threaten to unravel the fragile peace his father's rule had maintained. Entangled in a marriage with the independent Anya, he must navigate the turbulent waters of loyalty, love, and the relentless challenge she poses.

Amidst the cold sparkle of England's capital, alliances will be tested, and a new era of the criminal underworld will be forged as love blossoms amidst the chilling grasp of danger, binding families in a bond stronger than blood. With every life he holds dear teetering on the precipice of annihilation, will Nikolay rise as the don his father envisaged, or will the cold-blooded tendrils of the mafia claim him as yet another victim of its ruthless ambitions?

In this enthralling saga of love, power, and the unyielding grasp of destiny, every decision Nikolay makes will carve the path of the empire's future, for better or for worse.

If you are looking to escape into the fast-paced mafia world of stalking, secret identities, and deliciously heated arranged marriages, you'll get all that and more in the Volkov Bratva Romance Series.

This is an arranged marriage, kidnapping occurs and there is a mole in the organization so the hero and heroine's lives are in danger.

If you need to escape into the fast-paced mafia world of stalking, secret identities, and deliciously heated arranged marriages, you'll get all that and more in the Volkov Bratva Romance Series.

PREFACE

Welcome to the Volkov family. This is a series of three brothers born in Russia and their love stories. This series was amazing to write. There is an overall story arc, and each book ends in a HEA.

I hope you enjoy these handsome devils.

XO,

Zoe

ACKNOWLEDGMENTS

Edited by Partners in Crime and Cheryl Shackelford
Special thanks to my dedicated ARCs Joyce Beard and Maureen Riley, Jeanne Jabour, Claire Trickett, and C. Hill for helping with proofreading.

NEW PREQUEL

Prequel for the new series- Borrelli Mafia!

only at shopzoebethgeller.com

NIKOLAY AND ANYA'S PLAYLIST

Playlist

My Girl-Oskar Cyms
Nothing to Lose-Marien
Promise's-EMO
Don't Mess With My Mind-EMO
Beautiful- Michele Morrone
Give Me Some Love-TYNSKY

DEDICATION

Thank you to my husband, you are my rock.

CHAPTER 1

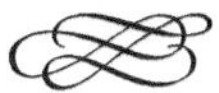

NIKOLAY

I park my black Porsche 911 Turbo S in the large driveway and greet my father's right-hand man as he opens the front doors made of glass and etched with our family crest.

Our estate outside of Volgograd is among the upper echelon of Russia. We enjoy a nice chunk of land, six bedrooms, seven bathrooms, a gym, and a theater. It reeks of something belonging to Los Angeles A-listers, only it's winter most of the year, and people dress differently.

The paparazzi are careful in what they print. Otherwise, they might disappear. Dad has more surveillance cameras than I can count. Most are hidden. I'm not convinced it is beneficial, as anything unsavory can be scrubbed. I think hundreds of years of subversion to keep an entire country under control won't be undone by modern technology.

"Good morning." Boris stands aside for me to pass. "Your father is in his office."

"Thank you." He gives me a weak smile before walking in the other direction. He has other duties to carry out for Dad, I'm sure.

Why were we summoned? We have no major beef going on with others at the present time. No blood has been spilled this year. Life has been good.

It is with trepidation I make my way to Dad's office. Mom is nowhere to be seen, another red flag if you ask me because she would never pass up a chance to see Roman. She was allowed to baby him, and he never went away to boarding school like Dmitry and me. We rag on him about it all the time. He's spoiled beyond what I call healthy. He pulls his weight nonetheless and is adept at carrying out missions we need covered without quarreling over them.

We don't waste our money on gauche items like the nouveau riche who pop up like weeds in our society. They are beyond ridiculous in their attempts to prove they are someone and belong in our world. They don't understand--we don't give a damn. New money isn't a threat to us. We have our closed circuit, and it's not changing any time soon.

We're entrenched in Russia's landscape like the Kremlin. However, I am not opposed to owning nice things. I have a weakness for fine-tailored clothing and beautiful women who are slightly older. I like maturity. Mama says I'm too serious. I know the Bratva comes first. I can't let my guard down, as I will lead it one day. Our family comes first.

My new leather loafers move silently over the Persian rugs in the hall. He must have been in here last night, no doubt sipping cognac as he smoked because a trace of a cigar lingers in the air as I approach his office.

I enter his lair with old books and family pictures crammed into the floor-to-ceiling built-in bookcase. A never-played chess set is on display between two chairs in a corner.

"Dad," I greet my father as he comes around his desk, and we hug briefly. Dark circles under his eyes confirm my suspicion he never went to bed last night. He returns to the large mahogany desk as I take off my coat.

"It's about time you joined us," my younger brother says from where he's sitting on the arm of a leather sofa near my father's desk. Even though it is worn and faded, my father clings to it for the memories we shared sitting on it when it was the only couch we owned. As kids, we were only allowed to watch American TV shows when Dad happened to be home. After he made billions, our lives changed drastically. I can't deny those were simpler, and honestly, happier times.

"Dmitry, I'm happy you could join us. I thought you would be visiting one of the brothels for your flavor of the week," I tease my younger brother from across the room. We saw each other a few days ago, working for the family business.

"Boys," Dad's voice commands as he plants his large hands on the desk with a jarring emphasis to get our attention before he sits. Our boss, and father remains still.

Immediately I stop cajoling my brother and find a spot by the window overlooking the pool and the grounds. Beyond the land-scape, the gray clouds are rolling across the sky.

Dmitry sits taller as if he's been scolded. I check my father's face for a read on the situation. Is he mad at us? It's clear from his pallid complexion he's tired.

"We are here on a serious matter. I would appreciate it if you would both behave." He looks to me, as I'm the oldest. "Where is your brother Roman?"

Under different circumstances, I would've continued to make smart-ass remarks because I love to push my brother's buttons. However, seeing as how Dad is clearly upset and in a black mood, I hold my tongue. Today is an example of the shitstorm world in which we make our millions. My guess is something terrible has happened or needs to be prevented.

At the sound of approaching footsteps, we all look to the door. The tile floors are made to look like wood, and it's impossible to make a silent entrance. Roman is so tall he barely clears the doorway, and his fitted jeans have to be specially ordered. His casual dress shoes are of no surprise.

He sheds his leather jacket and tosses it on a chair. "What's going on?" he asks. "I just got in last night," he explains while sitting beside Dmitry. He's picked up on the dour mood filling the room.

"Great." Dad's face relaxes upon the final arrival. Normally he's eager to see us and share his business dealings. However, today he seems stressed. "I have some news, news you might not want to hear, but it has to be said, nevertheless. Nikolay," his eyes find mine, "you should have a seat."

"What can be that important, Father?" I've been to this room many times over the years, and never has it been life-changing. Sure, I stayed out past my curfew as a kid. I always ran with the wrong crowd because we are the wrong crowd, and I don't apologize for it. Someone has to be able to step in my father's footsteps when the time comes. Dad always said it would be me. God, I hope he's not ill. I'm not ready to assume the responsibility of the family busi-ness. And I'm certainly not ready to get married, something expected of a don.

I sink into the large chair closest to our father. It's where I should be. I'm in command if he's not here. Dad sits in his leather office chair with his back to the bookcase. He's safer when he's nowhere near the windows. Traditionally, we associate drive-by shootings with America. Here, murders are made to look like accidents. It appears there is a use for retired, faceless KGB agents.

"First things first. One of my closest friends died yesterday. I only got word of it late last night." He gathers his breath. "My friend, Igor Petrov, ran a mafia organization in London, and it appears he got in with the wrong crowd. By the wrong crowd, I mean officials here in Russia."

Dad's voice quivers. I wonder if this is about losing his friend or something else. Maybe he hasn't told us everything. He's too smart to make a bad investment. My concern is growing as I wonder if we'll be affected by Igor's sudden demise.

Roman lets out a low whistle. Never, ever trust elected officials. Father's first rule of business was never to trust anyone, but mostly the powers of government. Mafias rose like wildflowers after the fall of the USSR, and we're independent of the Kremlin's reach. Do they want to own us? I'm sure the head leaders are chomping at the bit to control us, but my father has a network of loyal cronies who despise the ruler and help Dad stay off the grid. We don't want anyone to foil our business deals, nor do we want them to ask us for favors, such as stashing billions of rubles to hide them from international eyes.

Dad continues without commenting on Roman's vocalization. "Supposedly, he hung himself in his secure office building, but I think we all know better. I promised him years ago should something befall him—I would make sure his family is taken care of." Dad folds and unfolds his hands on the blotter covering the top of his desk. He turns to me, staring into my eyes.

All that's going through my mind is shit.

What the fuck have we gotten ourselves into?

"Nikolay, I need you to go to London. You are to marry his eldest daughter, Anya. I do not know if his enemies will target the rest of his family. However, I owe it to my friend to protect his firstborn child. You can see the rest of the family settled as you see fit. We discussed the two of you marrying at some point in time. I've postponed it for years to give you time to mature. You are thirty, and she just turned twenty-five, so it is appropriate."

"No," instinctively flies out of my mouth.

"What?" Dad raises his voice again.

"Dad, that is so outdated," are my last words, smoothing over the fact that I'm being disrespectful. He's Don Volkov. I am being rude even by family standards. "We don't do that anymore. Surely, there is another way we can protect the girl." She's the same girl I had a crush on when we were in school. She was the first girl to get under my skin in a way no person ever has. We had a connection. Where others feared me, she stood up to me and called me out for teasing her. It's been years. I wonder what she looks like now. We were only kids. I'm sure our crush was only that—perhaps she's met someone to love by now.

I snap back to the present. I have more important things to do. I can't be married. I prefer my women to be older, not younger.

"I'm a businessman," I say as I sit in the chair and lean over my bent knees to take in my father.

"That's exactly why you need to be the one to go. You are the one who will take over when I am no longer here. We need a larger presence and legitimacy in London. Marrying Anya will automatically get us in larger circles, and our Bratvas will be one. Together, you two can rule better than going it alone. Until your wedding, we need to protect our interests in London, and we will divest ourselves of our friend's ill-fated businesses, the ones which are part of whatever debacle he got himself into." Dad rubs his palms together as he shifts in his chair. "My friend's death was over his refusal to sell stock short and give up profit margins with an oil company he got into bed with last year."

I take a long breath. I didn't see this coming. Father is too smart to play with the political landscape. Our government is more dangerous than our rivals in organized crime. I slump in my chair with the news of Igor. Anya... it's been so many years since I've seen her, and memories I buried break free. I shake them off as Dad sits in his overstuffed chair, the type one would find in a high-end hotel, not a home office.

"I warned him not to do it. I went in on it myself, so I hope it doesn't affect me. I knew better, but he could be persuasive. The rumor is the government is raising money again. Maybe Igor didn't want to take a loss. They killed Igor to make an example of him, thus ensuring upcoming negotiations aren't met with resistance. I hope once you marry his daughter, everything will return to normal. In the meantime, there is no way Igor's wife can run the business. I've notified Liev you are coming. He's back in our London operation. He will handle our money collections and work with Igor's consultant, Konstantin. You will be poised to merge our businesses. We need to remain strong, son." His steely eyes, filled with fear, meet my gaze. "Otherwise, we'll have other nefarious organizations in London picking our operation apart, piece by piece. We can't risk a power grab; you know what happens next." His voice falls a few octaves as he remembers his friend.

"War," Dmitry interjects passively.

"I have a life here," I groan. Not to mention the relocation will mess up my weekend plans of sexual encounters at our private club.

"You'll take over our estate in London. It's massive. Take Anya there, have a wedding as quickly as possible, and keep it a secret. You'll be a target if insiders want the throne," he warns as he swivels in his chair so our bodies face each other. I catch a flicker of light in his eyes as he reminds me it's my duty to marry.

Sure, he hounded me for years, but thirty is still young. I thought I had a few more years of freedom before I was expected to carry on the family name. Forty looked like a good number, even if I was deluding myself.

"On your own turf, you can control security. Look for impostors. You need to be careful. Done correctly, we will send a message to our Bratva and our rivals. Anya is to be one of us. We're respected as we own our steel company and shipyards. You will clean up Igor's books. Any businesses with partners we don't want, we liquidate." His voice is strained as if his throat is constricted. I wonder what he's not telling me. He leans back in his padded chair now that he's delivered his message, and seemingly relaxes.

By delegating and shifting the burden to us, he's beginning to come out of the dark place he dwelled in when I arrived. Now, I notice color returning to his face. He seems sold on aligning our families and increasing our income. Done correctly, we'll gain more clout, increasing our power. I shouldn't lament the fact I have to be sacrificed for the Volkov Bratva, considering it will be mine someday. We were raised to serve.

Dad takes a handkerchief from his pocket and wipes his brow. I don't have the heart to fight him on this farce of a marriage idea. I'll go to London and try to find a way to wiggle out of the wedding once he gets over the shock of his friend's death. We were also raised never to show or give mercy. It's reserved for immediate family, and I utilize it now as a member of this family.

Marriage to Anya will be an arrangement. I'll never give my heart. It belongs to the Bratva. There is no room for love, only business. Even children are a business move because I will need an heir one day.

Contemplating my change in plans, I rub the overnight stubble on my chiseled chin. I'll have more time to think on the jet. No doubt Anya will be easy to push off as she's young and inexperienced in the ways of the world and bed as well. I've been told she's a virgin—a fact my father confided in me before I left him.

I hope she'll be subservient. I don't have time for a young woman who doesn't understand family business. If she resists me, I will change how I think about my cock regarding women. Making love is both a talent as much as it is an art. I happen to excel at both. One only needs to look at my house filled with my expensive art collection to understand I appreciate beautiful things.

I leave to pack for my trip to London. I pass Mom on the way out, and she promises to have some of my artwork in storage shipped to London. She mentions the mansion has been renovated this past year to prepare it for the day I would marry. It's woman's work, but she went out of her way to update the family estate. It's a loving gesture, so I thank her.

After tidying up my home and packing, I have dinner out with Pavel, my advisor, known as a consigliere in Italian Mafias. He is my trusted friend I've known since my teenage years. We met after I moved here from the small town where I was born. I fill him in on the upcoming changes and turn in for an early night.

It's been a long day, and a good night's sleep is needed. I crawl into an empty bed. I sleep alone no matter what; it's how I stay on top of my game and keep my emotions focused on business, not pussy.

The phone rings and jolts me awake at two in the morning. Nothing good happens in the middle of the night. As a made man, it's the time of night when death occurs, or war breaks out. I am reluctant to answer, knowing it's bad news.

"Da?"

It's Mom, and she's not making sense. Russian is rattled off like M14 bullets.

"Breathe. What is it?" Asking is semantics. If she's calling me, Dad is dead.

"Your father is gone. He had a late dinner. I woke up. He's not here. I heard someone say they were ambushed on the drive home. Your father was shot. Boris is dead too." Her voice wavers.

It's too early to know if this is an attack on the entire operation or retribution. Dad was not himself today. I've never seen him nervous. I assume he and Igor were in bed on a deal that went south. How could he not confide in me?

"I'll be right there. Don't move."

Fuck. I call my brothers to meet me at the house. We assemble in Dad's office, and just like that, I'm the king of the empire, the new Don. We go over assignments and live to see another day.

Morning dawns. Dad's body is cremated, and we hold a small service in three days. The Brigadiers and close associates join us in attending my father's funeral. The rain is fitting for the occasion. "Even God is crying," Mom murmurs.

We have a simple wake at the house. Mom is busy with food and has her share of vodka. I can't deny her the comfort of numbing oneself. I'm sure she blames herself in some way. I pay homage to the man who molded me into who I am today, even though I carry my sorrow in my heart. I'll deal with it later, maybe never.

There is no news of who ambushed his car. The local police don't give a damn. I'm sure they've been paid off, or it is a cover-up by the government; every elected official is corrupt. It's impossible to tell who has been paid to do what, not that it makes any difference. Dad is gone.

I resign myself to the fact my marriage is now set in stone. It makes no difference if the killer is found. Collectively, we agreed it must be linked to Igor, and Dad was involved or remotely attached because no one had stormed our or our men's houses in a bid to take over what is known as the Volkov Bratva.

As the pakhan, I put Dmitry in charge of our Russian operations, with Roman as our utility man to fill in where needed. We've increased the guards around the house. When no gunfire erupts, I assume the hits on Igor and Dad took care of whatever issue there was to settle. Life goes back to normal if this is what one calls normal.

We can't ask too many questions. Here, we swallow the propaganda the government officials feed us to not draw attention to ourselves, which would cause us to end up in prison or, worse—dead. In reality, we may never know the truth. I assembled the top echelon of the Bratva and my brothers, and we all agreed that this reeks of government retribution.

Dmitry is our tech man, and he might find something in the coming weeks to explain why our father is dead at fifty-two. Mama is having a hard time coping with the loss. They were in love as teenagers, and her heart was broken. She's taking sleeping medications prescribed by our doctor, who makes house calls. Our staff at the house waits on her, and Roman visits often, but she's reluctant to leave her bed.

"Mama, I have to leave for London. We need the alliance with Igor's organization to keep London solidified, and I'll see what I can find out. I know you'll always miss Dad. We all will. I must keep the Bratva going, so I'm doing my duty. You'll have a daughter-in-law in a few weeks. The family will grow if we stay united. Dad's death won't divide our Bratva."

Mom is always dressed to the nines, her hair coiffed weekly, so to see her as a shell of a person under the bedcovers breaks my heart. This is why I refuse to fall in love. It's not worth the agony when death eventually delivers the fatal blow. I swore to never love; I fear putting anyone in danger due to my stature in the organization. It's one reason I was happy Anya moved to London, even though I was pissed at her parents for taking her away. The wall around my heart is a fortress no one can break. Plenty have tried, and they've been disappointed.

What will it be like to see her again?

I stand, then lean over the bed. I hug Mom.

"I love you, Nikolay. Take care. I can't lose you too." The sorrow in her voice makes me want to stay an hour longer, but my obligations are elsewhere.

"I'll be fine. We're being vigilant. I need to reinforce our organization in London. It can't wait."

She nods. A true Bratva wife knows no one will hold her hand in a crisis. The Bratva comes first. Everyone is on deck to protect it at any cost.

CHAPTER 2

ANYA

Two days later, Mom still mopes around the house in a fog of grief. She's becoming an apparition; only a ghost would move. She's not. I wish she had more of a backbone. She's not one to assert herself, and because of this, I learned at an early age I had nothing to lose by speaking my mind. I wanted a different life for myself, swearing I'd never marry a man in the mafia.

Many arguments occurred with Papa, but he paid for my college education and a flat to get me out of the family house. I must have pissed him off royally. Blimey, father-daughter arguments are a pain in my ass. I can do without the drama. I'm sure it was Papa's decision I move out. It made his life easier even if he had to part with money. He hates doing that!

"Mom, you have to eat." I implore Mom to no avail. She sniffles, raises her handkerchief to her red nose, and blows. I'd laugh if I could; she sounds like a ship's horn, but under the circumstances, I'm sure we won't share a laugh for months. Meanwhile, Papa's body isn't being released due to an investigation because they are looking for further proof he committed suicide. Numerous investigators have inquired with us as to his state of mind. Konstantin warned us not to say too much, telling us the outcome has been paid for and if we make waves, we could be next to an unfortunate accident.

Papa is gone. Our guard, Sergei, sweeps the house daily for bugs. I can't help but check out how smoothly he moves about the room. I had a crush on him when I was younger. I like it when he smiles at me. He shouldn't, but he does when no one is looking. He's tall, with golden-blond hair. I find tall men attractive. I like the attention I get from him as Papa's less-than-stellar reputation kept men at bay. With Sergei, I have a male around, and never for a minute do I think he'd act on anything physically. Besides, I promised Papa to save myself for marriage in exchange for school.

The house is quiet without Papa's loud voice. He loved being in his office, talking loudly on the phone to show his importance. I suspect Konstantin, Papa's Bratva advisor, is preparing our soldiers for war because he hasn't been around today.

Papa kept us out of his dark world for our safety. My sister, Katerina, is not one to be trusted with secrets because she's immature for her age. She's into videos and posting the fancy food she eats with Mom on her social media accounts. I consider her to be more like an American teenager. However, she's twenty and isn't prepared for the real world. With Papa gone, our lives will change drastically. I wonder who will take his place as head of our Bratva.

Women aren't allowed to rule; it's a patriarchal society. We're to be seen, not heard. I feel like a character in one of those fictional romance books where only men can have power, and I resent it with all my being. I like breaking molds designed to keep the status quo.

The only information I have on Dad's death is from what is posted in the papers. If it's a hit, it will be covered up. Few governments want to admit to organized crime on their watch, even if many elected officials are on our payroll. The fact of the matter is they are on other mafia payrolls as well. That's why the truth of hits and turf wars don't appear on mainstream TV. I'm not naïve enough to believe Papa died by his own hand. I'm also smart enough to know I can't speak publicly without fear of retribution.

Mama says even the walls have ears, and I'm scared shitless. Is it over, or is there more to come? The Russian military has many mercenaries, and the government is known to use Interpol to track anyone adverse to popular opinions in the old country. I don't have to be told we're in a vulnerable situation. Members of the Petrov Bratva can't risk a threat from inside our organization—but it's usually what happens when a true successor, like a son, isn't there to fill the void.

Mama's voice raises as she argues with Konstantin on the phone, wanting an inquiry into the death, but he talks her out of it as it has already been ruled a suicide. Papa would never kill himself, no matter what darkness might befall him or his business. He wouldn't give up like a coward. He would never choose to leave us even though he often treated us with contempt. He was too vain to disfigure his face.

Papa was tough, making me use an alias for my last name in college to be safe because we live in Red Square. It's notoriously linked to Russian oligarchs. I've blended in well. My presence at school, and Papa's payments for it, depended on me keeping in line with his rules. When it was determined I seamlessly blended in, I no longer required a guard to follow me daily.

Now, the family name will be in the news, and everyone will think he hung himself in his office—my ass. America loves a low crime rate, and they love to hide the fact they let wealthy Russians into the country as long as they are willing to invest millions here as their ticket to freedom. Without the multiple billions Papa had, we would still be living in Russia.

The ironic part is how these Americans keep the patriarchal order and are themselves cogs in the government. How do they think we've all made this money in a communist country conducting legitimate businesses?

It's absurd, but it's what gains us unfettered access to the European and Western world. I find it repulsive that these two-faced politicians are often as corrupt as Papa finds in the underground world of criminals and thieves. It's as bad as it is back home. Only here we get to dress nicer and say what we want in public within limits regarding our homeland. But everything else is fair game.

And Papa's death? I'm sure I'll be told to stay out of it.

I relish that I can enjoy my life at the university and make a few friends. I'm such a nerd. I love homework and reading books on any subject. I find knowledge to be liberating and exhilarating. I'm close to my last year of law school, and I've managed to build a life for myself. I even go to clubs occasionally, and I've never been worried about my safety. I've made a normal life outside of my real identity.

The neighborhood is different after the news hits mainstream media outlets. Neighbors walk into their houses and ignore me as I pass them to go to the local grocery store. No words of condolences, no 'hellos' are exchanged. It's as if I'm tainted. I'm sure they're afraid to say anything for fear of repercussions. What is there to say? I don't know when or if I'll ever be able to enjoy being obscure again.

It's not the first time something like this has hit our community. Last week a family was murdered in Spain, and the explanation didn't fit the crime scene. A father would save his wife and unborn child, not kill them by strangulation before killing himself. They were on holiday for the summer. It doesn't paint the picture of someone orchestrating a murder. Strange how they were billionaires connected to big corporations in Russia as well. Is it a coincidence? Or is there a pattern? And if there is a pattern, what will happen to us? Will faceless assassins go down the line? Entire families have already been murdered.

I can't suppress a chill running up my spine and settling in my bones at the thought of how brutal these recent murders were; it's as if they are personal in some way, and it makes me incredibly thankful I've chosen a life outside of the dark one in which I was born.

I make tea and find Mum sitting in the blue and white living room. She dries her eyes. Konstantin arrives. Mum talks more than she listens, which is a shocker. She's not one to give her two pence on anything. Papa has her trained to be subservient. This is unusual.

I swear I'll never be quiet, taking orders without questions like her. It's the old way. I'm of a new generation and demand equality.

I'm sure the two-bedroom, two-bath flat Papa bought for me in the vicinity was purchased as an investment. Conveniently, it made room for my sister, Katerynia, who is spoiled so much at the ripe age of twenty that she has two rooms for herself. Papa has been working so much that he continued to buy her what she wanted, and now she's a handful. She has no idea what she wants to do with her life, and she has been in her room since Papa's death.

Mum rattles off in Russian before hanging up the phone.

"Anya, it appears we have help from back home. Nikolay, the son of your father's best friend, is arriving today. He's going to be your husband." She folds her aging hands in her lap, folding and refolding her handkerchief.

"What? I've never heard of this before. Why now?" Suddenly, my father's death takes a backseat to my future goals. "I'm in school. I'm not moving to Russia. I'm in England. I'm coming up on my last year at the university, and we don't need help," I spit the last word toward her in defiance.

"Anya, it was always to be this way. We didn't have the heart to tell you until the time came. And it's taken a long time to come about. However, the day has arrived. Why do you think your father bargained with you and gave you what you wanted? You must be nice to Nikolay." Her grayish-blue eyes warn me as she looks down her nose and over her black-rimmed glasses. "I am in a precarious position. I have to wait for the estate to be settled, and Nikolay can make our lives easier until our money is cleared, and we'll be safe with him protecting us. We need him to run the Bratva. The two families together are stronger. It will prevent a takeover and scrutiny of the government, which could land us back in Russia."

"This is ridiculous!" I stomp off. Now, I have something else to mourn: the loss of my freedom and my status as a single woman.

Sergei appears. He must have been eavesdropping, but he's our protector and member of the Petrov Bratva. He is sworn to keep us safe, but I doubt if he were put to the task against serious enemies, I doubt he'd be successful.

"Are you okay, Anya?" he inquires.

I glare at him; he doesn't deserve it, but he needs to be a guard. He's not a part of the family. If he had done his job better, Papa might still be here. Granted, he was not his bodyguard, but he is ours. I scan his face for signs of sadness, and immediately I'm sorry I snapped at him. He has a way of calming me when he knows I'm unhappy.

Normally, I'd trade pleasantries with him, but I can't today.

"Just fine," I reply gruffly as I grab my winter coat and purse to leave, seeking the sanctuary of my home. I can't be around Mum like this, and as much as I love my sister, she'll come around when she's ready.

I tug my coat on. I'm useless here. I'd rather be alone in my twisted grief. I loved Papa and hated him. The fact I have to marry a Russian turns my stomach. However, I know this is for the family's survival, and we need protection. Right now, my will to live outweighs my choice to choose whom I will marry.

I strike out on foot; the sky is dark. I wouldn't be surprised if it rained. I walk faster and repeatedly look over my shoulder to ensure I'm not followed. I assume someone who can kill my father in a secure building could outsmart me if they wished me dead. It's only now I wish I had a guard as an added layer of protection. I arrive home before the skies open; it will be a cold rain, and I have no desire to get sick.

Sure, Papa was distant, working on bigger deals until he was appointed CEO of a Russian oil company. I never knew why he was so driven when we had more than enough money and luxurics. Our home might be considered modest, but Papa is worth billions, judging from his holdings in corporations and stock investments. This doesn't include what he made off the books. It never occurred to me why we didn't live in a house in a more upscale neighborhood until now. I assumed Father didn't want to leave the area he had grown to love and where others surrounded him, all of whom conversed with him in Russian. I assumed it reminded him of his youth.

* * *

I unlock my door with a keycode and enter my flat, locking the deadbolt behind me as an added measure. My father's sudden death is making me paranoid.

I glance around my home to make sure it's empty before I can relax. The first floor has an open ceiling, as it was recently remodeled. A beam in the ceiling is the only separation between the living room and the kitchen. To my left is a loft on the second floor with a white wooden railing overlooking the downstairs area. The floors are oak, and cherry wood has been wrapped around what would have been corners in the narrow flat, giving it an updated look.

I have a gardening shed in my narrow backyard. My Volkswagen Jetta is parked in front of my two-story flat, with each unit connected. Where I live, there are rows after rows of them. Unless one has a house in the family for many years or makes a plethora of money, it's almost impossible for a single woman to own her own home.

I hang my winter coat on the wall hook and remove my ankle boots. I prefer to walk around without getting the polished floors dirty. I hate cleaning. Papa indulged me with their cleaning lady, giving me more time to study. My computer is in the loft, so I head up the narrow steps, reminding myself I can't fall behind this semester. There is no way I'm going to push off my graduation date next year.

No sooner do I get upstairs than the doorbell rings. I'm not expecting anyone, and I was set on letting it ring, but they won't stop. Ding, ding. I walk downstairs and peer through the front windows. Cameras with large flashes snap in my face.

I quickly dive out of sight and reach into my coat, pulling my cell phone out. I call Mom.

"The reporters are here as well, dear. Stay inside. Sergei is here, but you don't have anyone there to protect you," she laments.

"I'll play music to block them out," I say and ring off. I assume they will go away eventually. I sneak a look out the windows, and the media has taken cover in their vans. Those standing shield themselves under umbrellas as the rain pelts the rooftops.

I connect my phone to a portable speaker in the kitchen and return upstairs where I remove myself from the fiasco outside my front door. I'm in the midst of reading a textbook but jump when my phone rings again. I'm alarmed when I notice the area code to one from Russia.

Shit, shit, and more shit.

This can't be him, can it?

"Privet," I answer in Russian.

"Can you speak English, Anya?"

"Yes."

"This is Nikolay. Text me your address. I'm getting off the jet now."

"How do I know it's you?"

"Our fathers came from the poor small town of Uglich, and their first business venture was making magnets to sell to tourists in the cities."

"How do I know you didn't just look that up?"

"Because it's not online. Russia doesn't put anything on a computer they don't want to exploit."

He has a point.

"Fine." I relinquish my address. "And I have a gun. Just so you are aware."

I hear him chuckle before he hangs up.

I dive through my nightstand for the gun registered to my father. I'm sure I'd be in trouble for having it, but no one comes here. It's one of the rules Papa made me follow.

My hands shake touching the strong, sleek metal knowing it can take a life. I don't know if I could pull the trigger, but I assume I'd defend myself if it's my life or a killer's. I'm glad I don't have to rely on my street smarts to make a living because I wasn't raised like my father.

I carry it downstairs to the kitchen and throw a fashion magazine over it, hiding it in plain sight, so to speak. I learned that in a mafia movie.

I run back up the steps and take a quick shower. My heart is pounding. I have no idea what Nikolay looks like. I don't remember ever meeting him. We've lived in England for so many years I've not kept in touch with anyone from my old life. With my luck, he will be a fat, hairy Russian who reeks of vodka.

I towel off and blot makeup under my eyes to hide how puffy they were from crying earlier this morning, or was it in the middle of the night? It was dark when Mum woke me up.

I blow out my blonde hair with the hair dryer and about burn my scalp as I'm in a rush. When I've finished, I check my look in the bathroom mirror and add a touch of mascara to my eyelashes to accent my sapphire-colored eyes.

Did I overdo it? I don't want him to think I'm going out of my way to impress him. My business class ingrained in us one fact that I only have one chance to make a good impression. Subtle allure might give me the leverage to talk him out of our arranged marriage. I'm sure he doesn't want to be married any more than I do. It will be an easy sell.

I slip into my most expensive four-inch heels to make sure I'm not dwarfed next to a tall man and chuckle at the name Choo. It's a funny name because it reminds me of an old train, but it's great for branding. I carefully walk downstairs dressed in a top and fitted jeans. No sooner do I plump up the pillows on the couch when there is a distinct knock at the back door.

I race to it, wondering who jumped a wall to get in my backyard, and find myself looking through the peephole. I'm staring into the eyes of a stranger. He is holding a Russian chocolate bar like a white flag. Maybe he thinks it's his lucky day, and I'll fall for it.

Harrumph.

I open the door. "How did you get back here?"

"No, hello?" he chides me as he waltzes in like he owns the place, causing my jaw to drop. "You have quite the gathering in front of your flat. I jumped the gate." He hands me the chocolate. "It wasn't that difficult." He breezes by me and glances around my flat.

"Nikolay," I murmur.

He turns, and his long trench coat swings behind him, reminding me of Donald Sutherland in iconic movies from the '80s. Damn, if he's not impressive. Immediately, I hate myself for even considering the fact he's dreamy in a dark way. His brooding eyes don't smile, and he asks for something to drink.

I want to lash out. I'm not a maid, but I prepare him a glass of water instead, aware of his eyes on my butt. I squeezed into my skinny jeans and threw on a trendy sweater designed to slip naturally off one shoulder. The multicolor knit blends in with my dark orange bra strap.

I take three strides to reach the table and find him already sitting, my gun in his hands.

Holy fuck, did I open my door to a killer?

CHAPTER 3

NIKOLAY

I can't refrain from checking out my soon-to-be wife's curvy ass as she walks to the sink for my glass of water. Little Anya has turned into a woman, a pretty one at that. With each step, her heels click on the tile. I'm more interested in how her designer shoes lift her butt cheeks and fill out her tight-fitting jeans. Judging from her sexy off-the-rack sweater, her father kept her on a meager clothing allowance, and most of it was spent on footwear. Maybe she's not against our union, as I assumed. Why else would she dress like this? I wonder if she remembers me.

My cock twitches in my pants. She's sexy as fuck; my possessive growl is ready to erupt. I can't wait to sink my cock in her. She's mine. She doesn't know it yet, but she'll soon beg me to fuck her. Her honey-colored hair bounces behind her as she returns. I stifle a groan. It takes all my willpower to keep my eyes above her voluptuous tits when she turns around.

She must be aware of her effect on men. Why else would she wear a sweater showing cleavage and a bare shoulder? I observe how the color of it sets off her perfect, porcelain white skin, her rounded breasts on display. When she bends over to set the water on the table, thoughts of what I'd do to her set my imagination on fire. I can't wait to be sucking and nipping at her breasts and pussy. I won't be satisfied until she moans with pleasure under me. I envision myself coming over her breasts before I lick her pussy, reveling in her sweet juices. I'll relish the day she screams my name when she orgasms.

I chuckle at the gun she's stashed under a fashion magazine on the table and, having grabbed it, admire the fact it's been tricked out. A stealthy, reliable revolver with two barrels. She doesn't strike me as a woman who would own a gun, so I assume it's her father's, and she has it for protection.

"So?" Her eyes widen as I hold her backup plan in my capable hands.

She sits in a chair across from me, crossing one long leg over the other before nervously bouncing her foot faster and faster. The rhythm of her movement and my excited cock remind me I'm horny as hell, but I'm here on business. I never once considered the fact she might be drop-dead gorgeous. It's my duty to make sure neither of us gets whacked as I take my place as the head of her father's business before absorbing it into ours. It's dangerous not knowing if a takeover is being planned, but either way, there are bound to be some casualties.

Meanwhile, I place her gun on the table. "Nice piece." She could easily pass as a young woman. I'm not so sure I trust her when she says she knows nothing of her father's business—no doubt she can pull the trigger on a loaded gun. The girl has to know something, in my opinion. We all pick up more than we realize as kids. Plus, it would've been prudent of her father to make sure all the women in the house learned how to use weapons for self-defense. But that's just me, and I'm from a family of men.

"Thanks, it's my father's," she replies before she realizes she's using the present tense. His death hasn't fully sunk in. "I guess it's mine now," she adds wistfully.

I pause, realizing we both lost a father this week, but I can't get lost in the past. I buried my loss. It's what's expected of me. There will be time to mourn my loss later.

I take a few gulps of water to quench my thirst, but after I've drained the glass, I'm still thirsty. I'm in a quandary when I realize my real hunger won't be satiated until we're married, or I've fucked her. I'm sure the fucking will happen first. I have no desire to find her with another man. I assume she's still a virgin. It's hard to date when your family has arranged your marriage. And no doubt her father knew her every move. We didn't find a digital footprint on her, and I assume she has few friends. I've seen enough over the years to know how difficult it is to be a girl in a mafia family. She's a commodity.

"I assume you have heard of our," my voice is calm as I move my right hand through the air, "arrangement."

"Yes, only this morning. It occurs to me you can be anyone sitting here. I need to see some ID." Her eyes are stern but adamant.

"Mm," I murmur as I contemplate her request. Damn. She's right, I suppose. I'd be leery if I were a woman and my father was murdered, too. Granted, my father passed in similar circumstances, but because it was ruled an accident. It was a hit-and-run driver and a shooting considered road rage, now I wonder. However, we were able to bury him without a long wait.

I'm impressed she's thinking rationally when she's obviously under stress. Her sense of self-preservation is refreshing. "Fine." I stand, slip my coat off, hanging it on the back of a metal chair reminiscent of a '50s diner with a modern spin. I reach into my back pocket, tug at my wallet, and pull out my identification. I dangle my ID in front of her eyes filled with curiosity.

She slips her fingers around it, and I purposely hang onto it longer than I need to, causing our fingers to collide. A bolt of energy shoots up my arm, reminiscent of static electricity but more powerful. Immediately, I release the card so she can take possession of it, and she holds it like a chalice between her fingers, reading every line.

"Satisfied?" I sit again.

She hands the ID back. "One can't be too sure of anything these days. I knew Papa was into something when he started working longer hours. He was stressed. I never saw this coming." She sinks back into her chair and moves her leg to the floor.

"I'm sorry for your loss. It appears my father might have been doing the same. He was buried this week as well. The purpose of our union is to hold the Bratvas together," I state without emotion. "I have to focus on business no matter what emotional toll is laid at my feet; I've been trained to run it."

She nods pensively.

Even though I accept death in our business, it's never a good situation when our own has been taken. Granted I'm here to take over the Petrov Bratva with our men in London, having done joint ventures over the years, it's not a stretch. It was mutually beneficial for years, and we let Igor have a more significant presence here. It made sense to work together since we weren't rivals. Papa knew Igor was in trouble when he got into bed with people offering him too much money to take a job as the CEO of an oil company. Unfortunately, my father owned some of the shares in the same company. Igor got greedy as he grew older, and I wonder if my father did as well. Maybe we'll find answers when Dmitry is done scanning both of their encrypted computers.

"I'm sorry for your loss," she murmurs.

"Do you have any idea who might be behind your father's death?" I inquire politely.

"There is no way to know. He never shared work with us." She shrugs. "I wish he had said something."

"He likely didn't see it coming. It's the best way to kill, keeping the element of surprise," I add methodically and spin my empty glass on the table.

Her face stiffens. Perhaps I shared too much.

"Is that what you do?"

Her question catches me off guard.

I shift in my seat, move the empty glass away, and fold my hands on the table. "I don't discuss my work." I give her a wry smile. "It's for your protection and mine. However, we need to show a united front. We'll be wed in two weeks, at my estate here. It's a wedding gift from my mother," I add to entice her to accept. It's certainly better than living here in the burbs. Her apartment is livable, but her father was cheap because I know he could afford to give her more. This place is a dump compared to what I offer.

The Petrov coffers will strengthen the Volkov Bratva. Once we marry, we'll be powerful and feared here as in Russia. Granted, I'll have to relinquish some of Igor's businesses, like the dubious oil company and anything else that may have had to do with our dad's death. I want nothing to do with it or its owners. I could be on the kill list as I'm poised to take over, so I will divest all the stock and hope it closes the door on old business and any future bullets aimed at us.

"An estate? Two weeks to get married? I love living here," she protests. "I'm single. I have a life. I like eating alone, standing over the kitchen sink. I do what I want." She stands in front of me. Her chest juts out. She's a spitfire and clearly a virgin. Otherwise, she would use her body to get what she wants from me.

I twist my large frame to survey her living quarters. "You'll need to make some changes in your routine. I like a sit-down dinner. I'm sure we'll adjust. Your apartment is not suitable. My estate will be our home. It makes the statement we need to send. You'll have a guard to keep you safe, and I expect you to honor our family obligations."

"I can't bloody well have a strange man following me on campus."

"Whatever do you mean?" My voice bristles with disapproval.

"I go to the university; I'm going to be a lawyer." She perks up, her prior sadness disappearing for the moment.

"No wife of mine will be attending a university or working," I sternly inform her.

"I'm not giving it up. I'm almost through the program." She moves closer to me, and it's a power move, seeing as I'm sitting, and she enjoys towering over me as she makes her demands. "I'm not going to let a man dictate what I can and can't do," she replies emphatically. "I'm not my mother. I refuse to be treated as less than an equal in this preposterous marriage."

"Your father entertained your delusions. It's not the Bratva way."

"Screw the Bratva way," she huffs. "I didn't ask for any of this. My life was just fine until Papa died then you showed up."

I stand, using my height to intimidate her. I'm known for my keen sense of reading people. She's got spirit and sass. "You'll not disrespect me or the Bratva name. It's the Volkov Bratva now. Your last name will be Volkov. Forget any notions of the independent life you had under your father. Those fantasies are gone."

She flinches and takes a step back. She needs to learn submission. I might as well set the rules now. She wasn't trained to be a Bratva wife—because they know their place. This is why I like older women. They've matured and know when to give up a fight. They also know sex is used to manipulate men to get what they want. It's used as a currency in countries, particularly Russia.

"Fine, I'm Bratva too," she reiterates. "I have one year left, and I'm not giving it up. It's my ticket to freedom." Her words assault my ears. My little bird is looking for a way out of the family already. In fact, she's been planning it for years. Would she leave me at the altar? I quickly decide I don't want to find out.

She's in a gilded cage, albeit one with perks worthy of royalty. Her life is becoming complicated as she can't enjoy the freedoms she's enjoyed for years. Change is difficult, especially when we resist what we know must be done. It sucks I have to be the one to rein her in. However, I also have a duty to keep my future queen safe.

"What I say goes," I raise my voice. This school thing must be important to her. I have no idea why. She has me to take care of her.

"We're in a free society here, and women don't have to walk behind men," she spat at me.

"We'll see about that." I turn and shout, "Pavel."

The back door opens, and in walks my right-hand man.

"This is Anya. She needs a bodyguard vetted by you."

He nods.

"Anya, pack a bag for now. You're coming with us."

"Can't I pack and move in after the wedding?" Her eyes implore me, but it's useless.

"No, it's not safe, and you're to do as you're told. Go. Pack. We'll wait but make it fast."

Anya slips past us and disappears upstairs. Her heels bang on the steps. I'm sure she's mumbling her discontentment with each thunk.

"Quite the looker, and here your brothers thought she'd be doggish," Pavel jokes.

"Beauty is only skin deep. She has foolish notions of being equal to men," I mutter in Russian.

"She's grown up here, it's what she knows."

"We'll see about that." This schooling seems to be a sticking point for her. I will take care of my woman. It's my pride, and our tradition. For her to work would be considered an embarrassment for the pakhan. No matter how many times she bats her long eyelashes, I'll not have her diminishing me in any capacity. I have to admit her spunk turned me on, and my cock is only now returning to its normal state. "Besides, she was born in Russia. Our fathers really are from the same hometown. She'll have to adjust," I mumble to Pavel.

"Well, her father was one cheap bastard." His eyes take in her modest flat. I'm hoping her father wasn't being robbed blind. We have yet to delve into his business affairs.

Sooner than expected, Anya appears on the steps with a backpack on her shoulder, announcing her bag is packed. She leaves her luggage at the top of the steps for Pavel to retrieve.

I slip on my trench coat and head to the front door to retrieve her coat and purse from the wall. I peer outside. The press is still there.

"We'll have to leave out the back."

"I'll start the car," Pavel volunteers as he carries the large titanium luggage and holds his hand out for her backpack. She relinquishes it when she notices me holding her coat. She quietly slips her arms into it and drapes her purse across the lovely, delicate shoulder I'd love to kiss.

"Good," I reply, noticing her every move, "you might have to ditch the shoes. If the media discovers us, we're making a run for the car."

"It's wet outside." She furrows her brows.

"Maybe sensible shoes would have been more appropriate," I point out smugly.

Anya pulls her keys out, locks the door behind us, and we make our way to a wooden gate in the hedges. The walkway is covered in puddles.

"I might have to carry you," I murmur.

"I'm fine," she huffs as she splashes through puddles and ruins her shoes.

"Alright. Let's try to look like a happy couple in case the tabloids get a picture."

"I'm not interested in what the press thinks. It's not like I'm important," she replies as I slip my arm around her. I can't deny I like being protective of her as my eyes quickly scan the area for trespassers.

"That's about to change," I snarl. The Volkov name will become more prominent with me opening the family residence in London. I normally go to the coast of France when the leaves turn colors in autumn. The elite travel, enjoying warm weather destinations in winter. However, with an impromptu wedding, maybe a quick getaway on my yacht visiting the French Riviera will suffice for a honeymoon destination. It will be safer than sitting here while we figure out who Igor's enemies are. It's better to be a moving target if we're a target. Then again, maybe I'm being overly cautious.

Anya bristles as I pull her closer. I place my other hand over her arm to keep her in line. Just the way it should be. She'll learn how to be a Bratva wife with time. She's young. She'll learn to adapt. Young girls tend to be superficial and immature. They live on their phones and can't carry a conversation.

The familiar clicks of high-powered cameras hang in the air as we pile into the SUV. Pavel drives us outside the burbs to my sprawling estate. Undoubtedly, it once belonged to an Earl or the Queen herself.

"What will they do with the pictures?"

"Probably make up outlandish captions."

She settles back in the seat and accepts me sitting beside her without a fuss. "Woman taken by a thug," she murmurs.

I suppress my chuckle.

"Who is your father's guard?" There is so much to accomplish in a short amount of time. I hope Igor was smart enough to keep encrypted information in a safe place.

"Baran."

"Was he with your father the day—y' know?"

"As far as I know. Why?"

"Get on that, Pavel," I command.

"Sure thing." He maneuvers in traffic, and the SUV zips through roundabouts.

"Any other guards? I assume you have more than one?"

"Sergei, he's nice. He mostly stays at the house in case we need him. Why?" Her eyes beseech me to provide more information.

"I have to meet these people, and you are the one with the list of players on the chessboard," I reply smugly.

"Are they suspects?" she asks cautiously. Spoken like a dedicated daughter.

I turn my body to face her and remind myself her father just died. I need to give her time to process the loss and not give her information that will put her in harm's way. I keep busy to avoid dealing with my loss and wonder how Mama is doing back home. The wedding will cheer her up, as will the London scenery.

"I have no clue. Do you think someone is capable of being bought?" My eyebrows furrow together like two caterpillars kissing. Her gaze meets mine. My cock fills my fitted, overpriced jeans.

"I have no clue. I don't think so, but I didn't think we'd be going to Papa's funeral this week, either. Or that I'd be getting married." She shrugs.

"That makes two of us." I stare past her at the gray afternoon. It's fitting for my mood.

"We'll have a guard for you. You are not to leave the estate without me knowing in advance. Understood?"

"We'll see." That's not the answer I'm looking for, and the right side of my face buckles at her refusal to concede to the fact her place is beside me and in my home. "I hope I won't have to chase you down, but I will if you disobey me," I warn.

"I have commitments." She gives me the side-eye as if to challenge me.

"We'll talk later." I run my hand over my chin as I sit deep in thought. She's not the meek and subservient girl I imagined. I inhale deeply and inhale the faint smell of summer flowers surrounding her. It suits her features and evens out her disposition in her duress. "Hopefully, this will be behind us soon, and the wedding will cheer up your mother and sister," I say, changing the subject.

Why am I being nice? I don't give a fuck if anyone is happy. My life isn't about pleasure outside of the private clubs I frequent. We have some sex clubs in London. Maybe I can get my cock wet before the wedding. It's not a real marriage. I plan to keep Anya on the other side of the mansion to give each of us privacy.

"I don't understand how we're to go on," Anya murmurs pensively as her voice quivers. She turns her face to the window, so I can't see her expression or what I assume are quiet tears.

"You're capable of more than you know," I say, and it's my only consolation. Any other reassurances would be misplaced, in my opinion. "I'll protect you. I assume I've stepped into a hornet's nest. It's prudent to assume the worst and hope for the best." My voice is even in its delivery. I'm pragmatic. A leader can't be emotional.

I'm relieved my brothers will be here soon. I'm in a foreign country with a woman I'm to wed, and even though I'm the Don, it doesn't make me happy knowing it came at the expense of my father's life. It's a reality we rarely discussed when he was alive.

I wonder when we'll have kids. Obviously, I need to carry on the family name. Besides, there's no reason to have a son in the Bratva if they aren't trained to take care of the family business.

If we have a son one day, I hope he has Anya's fair skin and vibrant blue eyes. With my height and her high cheekbones, we'd make gorgeous children, maybe even models. God knows someone needs to mellow out my brooding temperament and give my sons a better-looking mug. Anya is smart. She'll serve me well in time.

From what I've been told, she's close to her sister and has a nurturing side to tone down her independent spirit.

I shake my head. What the fuck am I thinking about? This vixen is bewitching, and the fact I remember her from our childhood is disturbing. What is it about her making me crazy and possessive? It's not possible to meet one's soulmate when you're a teenager, is it? Do I even believe in love? Is it fate?

"I'll have your needed possessions brought to the house. You obviously blend in with the locals. You'll need other attire. It will need to be done soon. I've taken the liberty of buying some things for you for now. But you'll need to shop."

"I have classes. It's not so easy. And what attire are you referring to?" She sends me an inquisitive glance and pats the corners of her eyes with her fingertip. I assume she's removing dampness left by tears. Like me, she's back to herself, and her tone is edgy.

I questioned her fashion sense, and she was clearly annoyed. This isn't going over well.

"Clothing that's not so..." I flip my long fingers through the air. I want to say 'you,' as in sexy, with firm breasts and an ass I'd love to squeeze. Instead, I paused before I spat out, "Informal." I take a breath. "There will be events we'll need to attend for business. I'll need you to make introductions."

"I know who the players are from the tabloids. However, I don't circulate in those circles. Papa kept me and my sister away from it as much as possible."

"That will change to a degree. Maybe it would be good for you to attend school and keep your life as normal as possible. You'll have to have a guard with you for your protection. But there are obligations you'll need to undertake after the wedding. Charity work, social events..." I stop short of children. It's too soon.

"I don't need a guard; I don't have any issues. Most people have no clue who I am," she protests.

"I said you will have a guard, and that's final," I snap, tired from my flight and having my world turned upside down with one sentence from my father. An arranged marriage, huh? I can have any woman I want. Women drool over me and would love to have me as a husband, and here I am with the girl next door, literally. I don't think she remembers our past. She was the first girl I kissed, on the cheek, as she was so young. Her eyes looked into mine; it was as if we owned the world. Funny how it comes back to me now. Not that I could ever forget her.

"Ugh," she murmurs, twisting her body toward the car's door.

We arrive at my estate and stop at the wrought iron security fence. It's manned by an armed guard who keeps his weapon hidden, and he opens the gate.

Pavel drives past a perfectly manicured lawn and parks behind the house. Men wearing black stand outside the entrance to the back doors. I remain quiet as I stretch my legs, slowly walking a few steps from the vehicle. I take in the vast estate, and my mind churns. Who would have wanted Igor dead? Who would have the most to gain? It's not my duty to solve the mystery surrounding his death. However, I need to know who I can trust.

To further complicate my life, Anya isn't easy to forget, especially since she's grown into a beautiful woman. I need to remain focused on my job, but I find her to be more challenging than a poker game with strangers. She appears beside me, and I lead the way into the home. "We have staff, but you may need more," I announce as we walk through the vast kitchen and into the heart of the three-story house.

Mother made sure Hazel prepared the house for our arrival. She is an English woman who cooks, cleans, and manages the property.

She started out as a nanny when we visited England over the years and has been faithful to us.

My family has a presence in London, but we're more on the working level and haven't become as legitimate as Igor. I'll put it this way. We're not on Interpol's radar. Anya's family is in bed with politicians, soccer team owners, and billion-dollar businesses. It's not like I haven't been swimming with the sharks. Only my predators usually work the streets at night, not at fancy galas.

"This is beautiful." Anya pauses, taking in the opulence of the marble floors, the elegant chandeliers, the large white sofas, and the matching chairs in the living area. This is only one room out of many. I have fond memories of playing here with my brothers. Mama knew all along I'd be married and living in London. Her timing is always perfect. As promised, her renovations make the house more elegant. The atmosphere is elegant, and her attention to detail is impeccable.

"Come, I'll show you to your room so you can get settled." On the way, she discovers a partially open door.

"A library!" Her voice is full of glee. She loves to read. And if I had thought about the Anya I knew years ago, I would have shown this to her first. She always was the bookworm; it makes sense she's to become an attorney.

"You can use it. The office is off-limits."

Pavel remains downstairs as we take to the steps, and when we've reached the top, I lead her down the hallway to the other side of the house. I peek at her and her hair, falling in waves over her shoulders. I secretly inhale deeply to get a whiff of her essence.

I wonder how long it will be before I get to taste her lips, caress her skin, and make her mine. Heat radiates between us, and if this keeps up, there will be many cold showers in my future. I planned on keeping her far away from me. Now, I'm not so sure I like that idea.

Within hours, the tabloid rags have pictures of us online, and I'm labeled the 'mysterious, handsome man' who has come to her rescue. I snicker at their insolence in selling this horse shit to the public. Then again, most of the fair citizens don't want to know of my existence or that I work to clean the streets of many unsavory characters and make millions every year.

CHAPTER 4

ANYA

During the drive, I had time to study Nikolay, and arrogant is winning out as the number one descriptive for this incredibly handsome man who is to be my husband. He loves himself and is probably good at his job or whatever dark thing he does to make a living. In time, I will find out more, and it causes my belly to lurch with excitement and trepidation.

I never knew Papa had a contingency plan. This whole arranged marriage is the price to be paid to keep Mum and my sister alive. A sentence I must bear in the hopes my sister can marry for love. And considering the circumstances, things could be much worse.

Papa wasn't easy to stomach, always cutting me down and making me clean the house while Mum sat around all day watching soap operas. If it weren't for me, Katerynia would have dropped out of school as she was too lazy to do the class assignments. She's more of a social butterfly, and I'm the bookworm. Hence, law school is right up my alley between researching case law and writing briefs.

Father didn't want me to further my education. He told me it was nonsense and I'd never make it. He made me so angry I risked being punished when I talked back to him. I argued until he conceded and bought me the apartment to get me out of the house. In my own place, I felt normal for the first time in my life. I can't bring myself to the point where I'll trust men. It's safer to take care of myself and keep men, sexy men like Nikolay, at arm's length.

I texted Katerynia for updates on Papa's funeral arrangements. She informed me Sergei and Konstantin are helping Mum. I'm concerned no one has heard from Baran. Where is he? I assumed he would want to be at the house and make sure we're not under attack by rivals, but then again, they probably would have shot Papa in the street if it was an all-out Mafia war. Now, I'm thinking of conspiracy theories.

His death was made to look like it was by his own hand, so whoever killed him doesn't want it investigated. And that means there is more to his business than meets the eye. Someone sent a message. The largest question looms over us. Is it over? Or is there more to come?

I'm smart enough to know some London bobbies are on the take. Mafia and cartels don't exist without a certain amount of leverage on the justice system. It's in every thriller book I read. I love reading as life has a way of imitating art and vice versa. Today, I am reminded the real world is dangerous, and for a quick second, I'm relieved Nikolay is here. When I get overwhelmed by life, I retreat to my favorite books, like Little Women, where times weren't as complicated and arranged matches were commonplace, never dreaming I would be in the same boat in the twenty-first century.

Locking my door at night won't keep me safe. The lock is an illusion to trick me into feeling like I'm in control of my home. However, if someone in Russia wants me dead, nothing will stop them from making it happen. And for this reason alone, I'm relieved Nikolay and Pavel are both tall. If their muscles work as well as they look straining against the fabric of their dress shirts, I'm in. I've been naive to think a life of crime would pay. Life is easier when I pretend the darkness we live in doesn't exist. Today, I'm slapped with reality.

I was scared out of my wits thinking someone might be following me home from Mom's today. I tried not to look over my shoulder constantly. Is it so terrible to have a virile man taking control of my safety? I wonder what he's like in the bedroom. A man like him probably hangs out in sex clubs. According to the rumors on campus, it's the latest hotspot for the elite. The memberships are invitation-only, and the thought of what goes on there scares me.

I'm sure Nikolay has no problem getting women with his perfect nose, chiseled chin, and devilish dark eyes. My pussy is wet just standing next to him, but I'm not sure if I can handle his gruff and uncaring nature. His demeanor is rough and crass. He's a walking contradiction whereby he pulls me in, and before I take a breath, he's pushing me away.

How can I be angry with him for taking away my freedom when I get lost in his smoldering eyes? I can't get him out of my head, even as I enter my room, and he's nowhere to be seen. I can't ignore the tingling sensations between my legs as I contemplate being with him for the first time. What would his skin feel like if I rake my fingertips over his back or arm? I blush at the thought of him naked in front of me. Will he run his hands over my body? Will warm lips trail down my neck and kiss places no man has ever touched? Or will I be a warm pussy for him to get off in? He's sexy as hell, but it appears women are only objects to be ordered around.

He's a mystery. There is a familiar smell about him, something that reminds me of Russia, but I can't place it. It's from my childhood, this much I know. I went to school in our village, and he said our fathers were both from the same town. I wonder if we've met before.

Dropping my backpack and purse on the bed, I take in the room where I am to sleep and, I presume, study. It's familiar and inviting, decorated in blue and white, similar to my flat. The coincidence is astounding. I sit on the bed, and it sinks slightly under my weight. It's only now I realize I'm extremely tired. My day started after midnight, and the stress and shock take their toll.

How can I marry Nikolay when he makes me nervous with his steely eyes filled with contempt? I'm jittery around him. His intelligence is impressive. His tone is commanding. I find it turns me on, a man in charge and sworn to keep me safe. At the same time, he can be so irritating. No doubt he'll want me popping out babies for his Bratva. I never saw a man so in love with his brotherhood before today.

His bad-boy and broody nature piques my interest. He has a wall around him that makes me feel like he's off-limits, but the connection between us can't be my imagination. His eyes taunt me, and there is a familiarity between us I can't explain.

I gave up sexual freedom to go to school and study law, figuring it was a short-term sacrifice for a long-term goal. I've dated, just not seriously. I prefer to stick to myself and have one girlfriend, Darci, who is a bit wild. We only met this past semester in class. We complement each other; she gets me to venture out, and I reel her in when she's over the edge. She's from money, her father is a pop star, and she loves to be incognito because she used to frequent clubs when she was a minor. I've never looked her up online or been to her place. I've never met her family, but how many of us do that today?

Funny, I thought I had my parents over a barrel with the university issue. Now, I realize I played into their hands. All along, I was promised to Nikolay. That's why I was to remain chaste. I'm sure he's expecting me to be a virgin. Papa had his own agenda; he was always bargaining with me. Fuck him. He's dead, and it doesn't change how angry I am over the fact he played me and promised my future away without a word to me.

Isn't it enough he ignored me most of my life? Papa has an estate outside the city. I knew he could afford a nicer flat for me. Instead, he told me to be grateful for anything he gave me. It's another reason I'll never let a man control my destiny. If I have an education, I can make my own rules.

He treated my mother poorly, and their marriage deteriorated over the years. When he'd jet-set away for the weekend on business, I'd heard the guards talking about the parties he threw. I'm pretty sure Mum knew he was cheating on her, but what was she to do? One can't afford to live on a meager salary in this neighborhood. Mum never worked. She and Papa were from the same small village in Russia and married before they were twenty.

I stare at my phone and Nikolay's number before saving it in my contacts as Nikolay the Control Freak.

Nothing in my past could have prepared me for the butterflies in my stomach when Nikolay entered my kitchen. I find it disturbing how my body relaxes with a whiff of him as he passes me or the jolt I experienced when our fingers touched. The aura of mystery surrounding him makes me curious about his personality underneath the somber and, at times, the menacing face of the Bratva. I'm relieved he thinks foul play happened to Papa, and we both know it will be covered up.

I open my compact computer and am startled by a knock on the door. I guess even surrounded by security, I'm still on edge. I turn as the door opens.

Pavel stands in the doorway. "Your luggage," he announces stiffly.

"Thank you. What is the password to the house? I need it for the WiFi."

"You'll have to speak to Nikolay." He disappears.

This is ridiculous. Doesn't anyone here breathe without his permission?

I storm out of my en suite and head to Nikolay's, figuring he's gone there to freshen up after his flight. As I get closer, I can hear him speaking in Russian.

"I want Baran found, and you know what to do. No guard gets to live after that screw up."

Immediately, I'm fearful he'll find me in the hall. Obviously, I've overstepped. I backpedal, stepping backward in the hallway.

His door flies open before I can distance myself fast enough. Pavel brushes past me without a look or a word. Obviously, he has important stuff to do with those instructions. I wonder who pulls the trigger.

"What do you want?" Nikolay barks. How did he know I was here? He's in the bedroom.

I enter his room. His energy and proximity intimidate me. Without a buffer between us, my breathing is irregular. The room is the size of my entire flat, but I'm still suffocating.

"I need the password for the intranet. I have homework. The funeral is this week. I can't fall behind."

He moves to a small desk, scribbles on a note-sized piece of paper, takes four long strides, and hands it to me. The tension crackles like static electricity, taking me by surprise. He's impressive and intimidating. I attempt to take the paper gracefully, but out of fear of our fingers touching, I flinch, and the paper flutters to the floor.

"You're clumsy," he grumbles as he bends to pick it up. "We'll try this again." He hands the paper to me once more.

I take it from him, careful not to touch his fingers, and clutch the note like it's a life raft. The password is a vehicle to my independent life within these walls.

I turn to leave, wondering why my hand tingles. For some reason, I want to please him even though he is rude, just like Papa. He's short on patience and undoubtedly assumes I am a silly schoolgirl. I learned that Papa didn't like to be interrupted early on, so if I wanted something, I asked for it when he was distracted. He'd say yes more often than not to get rid of me, which left less time for him to hand out criticism.

"Thank you." I turn to go, yearning to get out before he can hurt me again.

"Dinner is at six-thirty. I expect you to be on time."

"Fine." I agree to leave as quickly as possible. Is this how it will always be? He gives me something I want and asks for something in return. Tit for tat?

I can't wait to escape his scrutinizing eyes. I wonder if Konstantin is working on my father's businesses today. No doubt Nikolay will want to review the books with him and expect me to know the itinerary for the upcoming seasonal events. It's May, so the botanical gardens will be the place to be followed by horse racing in June and soccer in September. I read online that Nikolay has a fancy purebred racing horse, so I assume I'll have to wear a fascinator on my head to be like the models in Vogue.

In the sanctuary of my room, I pull a few items out of my backpack and set my luggage on the rack in the walk-in closet. I was shocked to discover clothes in my size for everyday use and a few dresses with shoes to match. I pick up a stiletto and realize it's a shoe I longed to have one day. It cost over 800 pounds and is my size. How did he know? How did he have time to make my room perfect and purchase new clothes? The tags are still on them; my knees weaken at how much they cost. The huge closet in and of itself is a rarity in Europe. In the past, most Europeans didn't have a wardrobe large enough to justify a closet, let alone a walk-in closet. I'm beginning to see the upside to Nikolay's generosity and the perks.

I unpack my suitcase and place my clothes in the white bureau which matches the bed. Inside the drawer smelling of lavender, I find underwear and bras. My items pale in comparison to the new collection, and I'm embarrassed by my unsightly bras and unflattering undies. I shrug. Maybe I'll toss my stuff. Nikolay seems to have everything under control.

I log onto my school account, and before I know it, it's six and almost time to meet Nikolay for dinner. If I'm late, he'll be pissed, and I don't want to piss off a man who has no problem killing men who fail to do their job correctly, a fact I'm trying to forget, knowing it will be impossible. His father raised him in true Bratva fashion. Ruthless and domineering. It's dangerous for me to stand my ground with him. I don't want to end up missing.

I find a thick sweater in the closet, remove the tag, and pull it over my shirt. The temperature in the house has dropped since it rained. It would be inappropriate for me to show bare skin at the table. Based on the formal décor throughout the house, I'm guessing dinner attire is not pool attire. Nikolay is from the old country where only the wealthy can afford to eat prime cuts of meat, drive foreign or imported cars, and live in a large house without sharing it with four other families.

I make my way down the wrought-iron spiral staircase, careful not to trip while wearing my new shoes. I hope he finds me suitable. I don't want to have a marriage where I'm skulking in a corner. I refuse to be afraid of him on general principles.

The formal dining room chandeliers are lit and glistening. The gold trim on the porcelain plates reflects the soft light from the candles, giving the room a romantic glow. I've never seen such opulence in person. My breath catches when Nikolay stands. His designer suit reeks of all the money he spent on it. He gestures for me to sit next to him.

The table is decorated with a centerpiece of pink and cream roses. The table runner and napkins are embroidered with his family crest and beautifully tied with a silk ribbon. I've only seen elegance like this in pictures of movie stars' homes and weddings.

I'm underdressed but hold my chin high and refuse to let it show. Papa made me go to finishing school, a secret I'm ashamed to admit. We're not the royal family, but he acted as if we were, and now it might come in handy. Nikolay is suave; he moves with confidence, and it intimidates me. I can see him filling the role of pakhan with ease.

I recall Nikolay saying I need new attire. It's obvious I don't fit the lifestyle he expects. I wonder if I'll be allowed to wear denim.

Nikolay pushes my chair in as I sit. "Thank you for joining me."

Is he thanking me? Here he goes, winning me over with politeness.

I place my napkin in my lap, folding my hands over it.

"I realize you may have overheard me earlier outside my bedroom, and trust your loyalty is to me." His brooding eyes deliver a message leaving no room for questions. Even if I asked them, I'm sure I don't want to know the answers.

"Of course. Now is not the time to take chances," I murmur. "But Baran?"

"Have you heard from him?"

"No, it's strange. Did you hear from my mother?"

"No." His curt reply tells me the conversation is over. He nods to Hazel, who pours our wine before leaving the room. She returns from the kitchen with the first course of Russian food. I'm used to English cuisine, and I hope I will be allowed to make a list of food for our dinners.

"She's a mess. I don't know why. Papa cheated on her for years. They were estranged. I guess there's a low divorce rate in the Bratva."

I help myself as Hazel lowers the platter between us. I scoop food onto my plate and wait for the handsome man with a stern face to eat first.

"Very low divorce rate. Don't get any ideas. Our marriage will be real in every sense of the word. We'll need to go shopping. After the funeral, I assume your mother will help you plan the wedding?"

"I imagine she will."

"Small wedding. We'll have professional pictures for the paper to send out after the fact, as we need to keep it under wraps for now. My mother and brothers will fly in from Russia. I want this to be an intimate affair. Those invited will be on a list I give you, and it will be at my request. The marriage can't be put off, and we don't want to be a target. We'll solidify our Bratvas and become a power-house with incredible reach."

"Mm."

"Your father's top man, Konstantin, will drop by later tonight," he says between spoonfuls of borscht.

I don't care for borscht, but I take a few bites so I won't offend him. Mom raised me to keep an open mind with food. I decide to sip the black tea for lack of anything to do with my hands. Nikolay's presence is formidable, and even if his eyes aren't on me, I know he's observant of every move I make.

"Tonight, I'd like you to behave like we've known each other for some time. You've been out of the family home. I need you to convince Konstantin you are on board with our families merging."

"I will do what I can." I swallow my pride. I have no idea what game he's playing and realize I should work with him if I want him to do things for me. I've learned men expect something in return for favors, be it sex or kisses. Fucking appears to be a popular currency in the mafia if Papa is an example. I'm sure Nikolay will be the same, and I wonder when he'll force himself on me. I also wonder if he'll cheat on me.

"The men tell me he's ambitious. Would you agree?"

"I got the impression he wanted Papa to get involved with more deals. Papa was stressed, and I heard them argue from time to time behind closed doors. Mom might know more."

"Mm." He takes a bite of his food, and I notice his elbows never touch the table. I wonder what his mother is like. It's odd. I like elbows on the table when having tea with a girlfriend.

"Why? Do you know him?" I attempt to gather information.

"Not exactly. Did you get your classwork done?" The fact he remembers our conversation earlier shocks me. I didn't think he was listening to anything I said.

I remind myself I'm part of his new business venture.

"Yes, thank you," I murmur. He barks orders like I'm a dog, and now it's all fine. "I like to stay at the head of the class," I add.

"I'm not surprised," he replies as more food arrives and, thankfully, my mouth waters for the pierogis.

Silence follows until his phone vibrates in his trousers, and he excuses himself to make a call. Nikolay's eagle eyes are on me, and he takes a second to remind me I'll be needed later.

I take this as my excuse, and after I wolf down the rest of my food, I walk up the staircase, half expecting to find an iron throne at the top. There must be an elevator, no? I glance up and see another floor over my head. I make a note to explore the rest of the mansion another day.

I lie on my bed and stare at the high ceiling. How can I get out of the marriage? My sister is too young. Maybe the uncertainty in the Bratva will pass and make our union unnecessary.

Who am I kidding? In the Bratva, the winner takes all. Papa took over when his father was murdered, and here we are, back to the same spot, years later. I have no doubt there will be a power grab. Marrying into a Bratva family who is stronger on Russian soil is the best route to circumvent an internal war. I don't know the business's day-to-day operations, but I know this to be true.

Voices float in the air, and when I open my door, Pavel appears in the doorway. Where did the time go? Nikolay infiltrates my every thought. No doubt Pavel is here to summon me downstairs.

We enter a living room where vodka is being poured. This is another area I haven't seen. The front windows are circular, so they must be at the front of the house. The ceilings are exceptionally tall, with recessed lighting. Even my friends growing up didn't have homes as lavish as this. His family is a prominent one to afford this.

"There you are, krasotka." Nikolay walks toward me and gives me a warm kiss on my lips, which lingers enough to make me wet. As soon as I experience his warmth, I assume he is warming up to me. But he abruptly pulls away, leaving me hungry for more. His chocolate eyes meet mine briefly before he is back to business.

I force a smile on my face and try to make it mean something.

Konstantin is still standing and gives me a kiss on each cheek. "Anya, so sorry about your father."

"Thank you." I sit as Nikolay hands him a short glass with a generous amount of vodka.

"I had no idea you two were together or serious," Konstantin mentions as he takes a sip of the alcohol before he sends me a quizzical glance. "I assumed you were in touch with your father, but he never mentioned this." His voice conveys his surprise.

"I've been out of the house for some time." I meet Konstantin's hazel eyes, not sure of either man's motives. He shrugs as if it's immaterial. "Papa and I didn't see eye to eye on much. I'm not surprised." I move one of the light blue throw pillows and sit on the off-white curvy sofa.

"I finished the funeral arrangements. I'm told the death won't be looked into. I'm sure we all expected that," he adds as if it's an excuse for something.

"Do you have his list of contacts?" Nikolay asks as if it's normal for him to know this.

"I can get them to you. I know your man, Liev, is collecting for you. I assure you I can handle my duties."

"I'm sure you can. However, there have been shortages, I'm told. I'll be taking over as Anya and I are to be wed. It will be a small affair; only you know the meaning behind the dinner invites going out shortly. Our families go back to Russia, and I want to make sure you're on board. I'll keep you on as my counselor, but I also have my own advisor, you understand."

Nikolay delivers the demotion smoothly. Now I know why he wanted me here. I'm a pawn for him to take over my birthright.

Not that I want to run it, but I'm the blood by which power will go to the Volkov family. My father had no sons to carry his name. The ties to my father's past spent in Russia weren't left behind with our home. Dad was thick as thieves with contacts back home. It makes sense. I'm sure his associates all served a purpose. Far be it from my father to keep anyone in his life who didn't serve his purpose.

I wonder how long I have before Nikolay wants me popping out blue-eyed Russian babies. It's the oldest trick in the book to keep women subservient and compliant. Women in Russia live in a repressive society, and I don't care what luxuries Nikolay can afford. I won't give up my voice to be with him.

Konstantin is older than Nikolay. His hair is slicked back and graying at the temples. His eye twitches as he realizes he's been outplayed tonight. He gulps down the vodka to help the sting of defeat.

"I understand. I met with Pavel. I assumed there was a contingency plan in place. Igor alluded to a will."

I'm not sure if he's saying this to put Nikolay at ease or if he knew what was to take place should my father die. I don't know who to trust.

"Is there anything I can help you with?" he asks Nikolay.

"For now, we're good. Thank you for taking care of the funeral arrangements. I'll make sure you are compensated for your loyalty," Nikolay replies guilelessly. It's as if there is a conversation within a conversation. "We'll meet after the funeral, and I would like an accounting from Liev and a list of all our obligations."

"Consider it done." Konstantin stands, taking this as his cue that the short interview is over. I notice his suit is worn by top Russian businessmen, and it's more expensive than Papa's, judging by the trademark horsehair stitching. I know, as I love to ride horses and the suits are made in London. I may not wear many designers, but I read about them in notable fashion magazines. It's my one indulgence, paying for overpriced magazines with pictures of jewelry, purses, and clothes I'll never be able to afford.

Until now, apparently.

My mind should be on my next class assignment. However, I love this room and can't wait to explore the other floors. I'll wait until Nikolay has left for work tomorrow. I'm sure he'll be leaving the house in the morning. A Bratva Don never sleeps.

I stand when Konstantin rises. Nikolay pours another vodka from the serving tray on the circular coffee table between us. The room has another modern couch, a sectional made of fabric matching mine. Stuffed ottoman chairs are scattered around the room to accommodate more people. I assume this room is to entertain guests and wonder if we can have guests and make friends. For a moment, I think of the possibilities of being a couple, of meeting others our age, and going to dinner parties and meeting at plays or famous restaurants where the prices aren't listed on the menus.

Nikolay observes the older man giving me good wishes for our engagement.

I thank Konstantin before he turns to my fiancé. "I assume the wedding will be soon?"

"Yes, I'll fill you in after the funeral; to speak of it now would be inappropriate. We are keeping it a secret until the dust settles. I'd appreciate your support."

Konstantin nods. Nikolay steps forward, the two shake hands, and it's as if they are new partners.

"You might want to put a ring on it, Nikolay," Konstantin murmurs, his Russian accent making waves in the room. Rich Russian women are similar to the women in the Italian Mafia. They like their shiny jewels, bright colors, and anything with a designer label.

Pavel walks him out. I turn to Nikolay. "What are you fishing for?"

"I needed to get a read on him. I'm testing him to see if he mentions the wedding to anyone or if he can be trusted. I'm trying to decide if someone inside your father's organization is on the payroll of an enemy or if there is dissension within the ranks. My goal is to figure it out before more bodies end up in the morgue."

Saliva slides down my throat like sand. More bodies?

I shiver. I never asked to be involved. And yet, here I sit, asking difficult questions without easy answers. Instinctively, I trust his judgment on all things Mafia.

Papa's death could leave a power vacuum that would tempt many to take over our territory or, worse, us. Papa mentioned the Irish are more active lately, and he was anxious about the races opening this fall.

"A drink?" I'm not sure if he's asking or telling.

I observe his calm demeanor. Meanwhile, I'm a wreck. "I'll take a vodka."

His slender fingers tip the bottle, filling another glass, and he hands my drink to me. I'm determined not to drop it as I confidently take it from him. Consequences be damned. I need to send a message of my own. I won't shirk from him. If I'm to be his equal, I have to fake it until I can escape. Each day I spend here takes me closer to my future with Nikolay. I can't deny he consumes my thoughts, and being close to him makes my panties wet.

The home is swoon-worthy, and I'm becoming accustomed to Nikolay's brief but approving words. I can't wait to go shopping and use the swimming pool Hazel mentioned. My tabloid magazines were my escape from my repressive world. Now, I live in the lap of luxury, and it would be so easy to give up my old life and align myself with Nikolay. I can assume my role as his wife, but I refuse to be silent where our marriage is concerned.

I throw the liquor back. It's smooth. I swallow it like a pro. This is where my nights of clubbing pay off.

CHAPTER 5

NIKOLAY

*A*nya retires for the evening. I move to my living room with the darker grays and settle on my favorite couch. I remember Mother asking me what I wanted in this room. I thought it was a surprise for Dad. We're so similar. I was the perfect person to ask. I have a minute of sadness at the loss of my father. I never wanted to become a leader this way.

The fact remains that I'm the oldest, and I've taken over as head of the Bratva. I'm a king in another country, but in time, we will network Russia with England as we solidify a more international network.

I pour myself a cognac, only the best. I stare out the picture window overlooking the massive backyard and take a sip. Looming to the right are rounded glass walls enclosing the pool, which enables us to use it all year long. With the price of electricity, it makes quite a statement. I wonder when my parents decided to give me this palatial estate. Maybe it was planned as a wedding gift.

It's the best area to raise a large family, with private schools, international cuisine, and cultural events. I take another sip as I notice the lights along our high gates and return to my favorite couch, where I kick my shoes off and prop my feet up.

"What do you think?" I look to the door as Pavel's soft-soled boots and limber build fill the doorway. He enters the room and pours himself a vodka. He's perceptive. Otherwise, he wouldn't be my advisor. He's also in charge of the spies we have placed in the cities where we operate. We have many within our organization, and I hoped he would have turned over a stone by now. But alas, nothing.

"We're flying blind. I'll feel better when your brothers arrive," Pavel replies with his calm and steadfast voice before he drinks the shot. He slams the empty glass onto the glass table and lifts the bottle to his lips, draining the last drop.

"It will be nice having them around. Who do you have to guard Anya?"

"Alex, he's an enforcer and Liev's friend. He grew up here, and he's a worthy choice because he knows the area, and I trust him." Pavel's grave voice matches my somber mood.

"I like it. It will get him off the streets for a while. Why don't you send someone to check on Baran? Go by his flat, see if he's around," I suggest. My eyes are tired as I walk to the bar. I fill a rock glass with Cognac. I found it hidden in here earlier. My dad was probably the last person to touch it. My mind segues and wanders down memory lane, but Pavel's voice brings my focus back.

"I'll get right on it." He clears his throat as if to convey his sympathy. I'm sure Dad is on his mind as well. He opens another vodka from the liquor cabinet, stands over the coffee table between us, and takes a belt. "If that's all, I'll arrange for Alex to be here tomorrow morning to make sure our little bird doesn't get any crazy ideas of escaping." I return to the room and sit on the sofa.

"Don't worry. She won't be running home. I don't think she had the life befitting a princess. I get the impression she's not a fan of her mother. Anya is a young woman with potential," I muse, wishing I had a cigar.

"And here we thought she would be easy to pacify."

"I'll take care of her and let her attend the university if it makes her happy and keeps her from running off." I swirl the amber liquid in the rock glass. It's been a long day. It's time for me to turn it in. "No alarms have gone off. I must be doing something right," I joke. Then I find myself wondering if she's sleeping and how she will look naked under me and in my bed.

Hazel pops in to clear our glasses and the empty bottle, placing the Cognac in the wet bar where it belongs. Damn, if she isn't efficient.

"Anything else, sir?"

"That's all, Hazel, thank you."

She nods her head to acknowledge me. She reminds me of my great-grandmother, only Hazel has a British accent. She goes about tidying the pillows in a chair before retiring to the vicar's cottage behind the house where she lives with her husband.

I walk up the steps, the endless steps in the four-story home, deciding to forgo the elevator hidden at the back of the house. It is fit for a king— oddly, I'll have a queen. Anya will need to take over the management of the property and create menus. Hazel knows what to do, but I'm sure Anya will enjoy giving a few orders of her own. I smile as I plan to give her the illusion of the independence she craves.

Anya is driving me crazy. She's nothing like the women I frequent at the club. My cock fills my pants before I reach the first landing. Does she remember us, I wonder?

She's a virgin, and she's mine. I haven't decided when I'll pop her cherry. I never go long without getting laid. I have no intention of changing my views on sex to accommodate one of celibacy and innocence. There is no way we'll share a bedroom; I'm not breaking my one rule on intimacy. No matter what I might feel for her, I won't let love through my heart of steel. It will be his and her bedrooms. No pillow talk, no favors, nothing to weaken my resolve to be a great leader of men.

I strip and slide between the sheets on my overly large bed. I tuck my hands behind my head and stare at the ceiling. The room is so dark I can't see my hand in front of my face. Anya is a modern young lady who thinks she can protect and provide for herself. I respect her working to make her life different from her mother's. Regarding protection, I hope she'll learn how vulnerable she is being associated with me.

My cock makes a tent, even with a heavy blanket covering it. I need to fuck her silly. Maybe it will give her a dose of reality and tame her. I'm in control. She needs to get used to a world dominated by men. By that, I mean me.

* * *

My cock is hard, and my balls are tight. I fantasize about Anya sucking on it. I can't entertain the thought of her being down the hall. I hop out of bed, deciding I need to keep myself busy, and take some laps in the pool to work off my sexual frustration. I make my way to the recreational floor, passing two rooms meant to house numerous guards who stay on the premises. Even with a bullet-proof front door, I'm playing it safe. Only time will tell if I'm on someone's hit list.

After an hour of laps, I sit in the sauna for a spell before I grab a thick towel. I dab my face and spot-dry my torso before wrapping it around my waist. I casually make my way to the stairs with only the damp cloth covering me as I enjoy the freedom of freeballing it. It's my house, and I'm enjoying my new domain. I'm the king of the castle.

I saunter into the foyer, intending to shower and prepare for the day, when I catch Anya ducking into the kitchen. My heart beats like a drum in my chest. I want to see her. I casually enter the kitchen, warmed by Anya as she talks to Hazel like they are best friends. I wordlessly pour hot liquid into a cup. I don't need tea, but I pretend I do. Hazel is making breakfast. Anya appears uncomfortable as she sits on the marble island in the center of the room.

"What's troubling you, Anya?" I can't bear my little bird's somber face.

"I'm not used to being waited on. It's weird. No offense, Hazel." Her eyes move quickly to Hazel's warm face to apologize for any slight.

"None taken, dear." Her pale blue eyes are soft— she likes Anya.

"I was the one who took care of everyone," Anya mumbles with a shrug.

This feeds my premise Anya wasn't happy at home. My heart pitter-patters with empathy. A child who wanted respect and recognition from their parents who managed to never see her for who she was. It's a shame. She'll be treated better here; I'll see to that.

"Enjoy having Hazel and hire any staff you two need. I meant to tell you that you are the lady of the house and can take over running it. Hazel will help you, but I'm confident you'll figure it out." I sip the hot liquid and lean against the countertop opposite her, totally unaware my towel isn't long enough to cover the boner I pop as I check out her cute yoga outfit with a zippered bra top and a cut-off jacket, neither of which cover her navel. I know I will fuck her sooner, rather than later. I hope she can keep up.

Anya's eyes grow wide as she notices my needs sticking out egregiously in front of me, and we both realize that neither of our sexual needs is being fulfilled. Her body is facing mine, and desire shines in her eyes.

Her voice trembles. "I'm to run this mansion? I'm not sure I can do that."

"Don't underestimate yourself. I believe you can. It's your home, our home. My mother decorated it to the best of her abilities, not knowing what we'd want, but do what you want. If you require a huge change, such as remodeling or new furniture in some of the rooms, we'll talk. Otherwise, I want you to make it comfortable for us, functional, you understand." I observe her surprised face and grin behind the cup at my lips. This will keep her busy and build her confidence. Maybe including her will make her less likely to run, and hopefully, it will bring her closer to me and my family.

I take a sip of my tea even though it's boiling and excuse myself. She's not a true conservative Brit. I have no clue where she got her Americanized flare for showing skin. I purse my lips together. Maybe the university isn't harmful after all.

I shower and dress for a formal day, choosing a gray suit, light blue dress shirt, and Italian loafers. The doorbell rings, and I listen as Pavel and Alex enter the foyer. The marble floors are beautiful and keep the house cool in summer, but sound travels.

I exit the steps and make my way to the kitchen, pop my head in, and address Anya.

"Dress. We have a visitor."

"What do I wear?" She panics, her eyes searching my face for a word of advice. Her mother didn't properly train her to fulfill her role as my wife. Otherwise, she would already know this.

Her mouth opens, then closes as if she were about to protest about changing. Apparently, she thinks better of making a retort. Part of me wishes she sassed me, and I smirk because I have a few toys in my bedroom she might enjoy.

"Anything but what you currently have on now. I suggest you only wear that outfit in the gym downstairs. No need to distract the guards. Come into my office as soon as you can." I step near Hazel and snag a warm scone off a cooling rack before joining the men waiting for me. I learned from Dad how impressive it is to not hide in an office and hand out orders. At times, I need to mingle with my top men. This is a civilized world, and, as such, we conduct ourselves to fit the occasion, but today, we're meeting here because I want to keep an eye on Anya. I love watching her facial expressions. She makes me smile, not that anyone would know.

"Bad news," Pavel greets me off the bat. It's business first, pleasantries later, apparently.

"No good morning?"

"I wish. There isn't anything good about it," he replies.

"So early, pray tell, what the fuck has happened?" I slide into my oversized chair and motion for the men to sit. Pavel leans against the built-in bookcase. No doubt Anya would be ecstatic with all the law books in it as well as classics; some are first editions.

I glance at Pavel, who is six-two and wears his long, black hair in a man bun. My father would have cut it off himself, but what do I care? He's a good man, and we've known each other since we were teens.

Pavel's hazel eyes meet Alex's.

"Baran is dead in his apartment. I just left the scene; his phone is missing. I assume he must have called in early the day of Igor's murder, hm… death." Alex amends his statement and checks my face to make sure he made the correct move.

I nod.

Until we're told otherwise, it's not wise to spread rumors that may reach the ears of the men who killed Baran, and possibly Igor. No doubt, many investigators are covering the "non-event." There is no need to put ourselves in the line of fire. The tabloids will run with what they are told, and it will blow over.

"Liev speaks highly of you," I comment with a hand on my desk. I take a bite of the scone and its sheer perfection, similar to how I presume Anya will taste when I bury myself between her legs.

"Thank you, boss," Alex replies with his English accent, drawing out the 'o' sound. He's no slouch, standing over six feet tall and all muscle. It's safe to assume this from his inked hands and tattoos, which I presume cover his body. Even though he's wearing a long-sleeved shirt for today's unofficial interview, I know Bratva men. He's from the rough end of town, where we move tons of product. He's old enough to be a seasoned soldier.

Anya taps on the door frame right on cue.

"Anya, come in." I stand out of respect, and so does Alex. "Anya, this is your new bodyguard. You are to go nowhere without him until further notice. Is that clear?"

She looks over Alex, his dark hair, dark eyes, and legs spread slightly to make room for his muscular thighs.

"If I must," she sighs. Her quick agreement has me worried. What is she contemplating?

Alex extends a hand and formally introduces himself. "Please give me your schedule. I'll make sure we're cleared to go."

"You're driving me?" Surprise rings in her voice.

"Of course, ma'am. How else am I to keep you safe? Can you do a pit maneuver?"

"No," she says without blinking or looking away.

"I need to be able to keep you out of harm's way. One needs practice to act quickly. I'm that person."

"Fine." She hands him her phone. He enters his information. "I'll text you later." She turns to me. "Are we done?"

"Yes," I speak for us all.

She turns as Pavel enters. "Good morning, Pavel," she says, giving him a megawatt smile.

"Ma'am."

She exits without haste.

"What was that all about?" I ask.

"No clue." Pavel runs his hand over his neck. "I'm too old to know what kids are thinking nowadays."

"Be on your toes," I instruct Alex. "You'll need to work with the staff for our secret wedding next week. Tonight, we have a service for Anya's father. Please don't mention Baran. We'll see how this plays out."

Alex nods and is excused. No doubt he'll be checking in with my future wife. It's one less task on my plate.

* * *

After a quiet dinner at home, we meet her family at the church at seven for a mass. My security team is conducting surveillance on the guests. I anticipate a few billionaires with English citizenship showing up out of obligation.

Anya stands close to her mother and sister. With everyone dressed in black with grim faces, it's the epitome of The Nightmare Before Christmas. Sorrow surrounds us; fear permeates the air. No, our friend did not off himself.

Katerynia is five years younger than Anya. They share the same blonde hair, wear it long, and look so much alike that they would easily pass as twins.

CHAPTER 6

ANYA

I join Nikolay's side at the wake. I am startled by his apparent jealousy over Sergei. His eyebrows furrowed as his jaw tightened. It might be my imagination, but I swear his body relaxed with my presence. And here I thought I only irritated him. He slides his arm through mine as he leads me around the room filled with strange faces. These are men of the Bratva, and they nod their heads out of respect for the king. There is a hierarchy, and because of it, Nikolay's face is not known to all of the men under him. In society, he is a legitimate businessman looking for connections or using partners as covers for his dirty deeds. Like the cold fingers of a witch, a chill eerily riffles through me as I observe the somber occasion and the vibe coming off the men.

We come upon my sister, and he pauses. I hug her. Mum is talking to friends of the family, ones close enough to be part of her social scene, and by that, I assume the inner circle. Many of the people are my mother's neighbors. I suspect some are Papa's business associates. I can't imagine what these men do for a living. They don't wear labels; it's left to my imagination. Is one of them responsible for my father's death? Will someone challenge Nikolay?

"How are you, Katerynia?" My sister wraps her arms around me. I'm sure she's had to step up and help Mom now that I'm not around due to my new jailor.

"I'll miss Papa, but he'd want us to go on." I attempt to cheer her up as her eyes are puffy from crying. I'm marrying Nikolay, and he's all we need to retain the criminal syndicate. She has a life of freedom ahead of her; I doubt she has a clue about the sacrifices I've made for her safety.

Katerynia gets to marry whom she chooses, and I hope she doesn't rush into anything. I want her to wait and make a good choice so my efforts to give her a normal life aren't wasted.

"I'm sorry for your loss." Nikolay's stern voice is on autopilot, yet his tone is as sweet as honey, putting me at ease. I doubt the man has an inkling of what the word empathy means. Perhaps it's the toll of exhaustion catching up to him. I can't shake the thought of Baran lying dead and the order he gave Pavel.

"Thank you, Nikolay. I hear you'll both grace us with a happy occasion soon." My sister resumes her stoic posture, her face composed.

"Yes, I hope you'll have time to help Anya plan a small affair."

"Of course, we're sisters," she exclaims, and her face lights up. In the darkness, there is light, another reason for a wedding amid the gloom overshadowing us.

Arranged marriages, huh? Is it possible I'm better off with him than taking a crapshoot with another? Sergei looks more like a movie star than a member of the Bratva, with his dark brown eyes hidden behind aviator sunglasses. He's slick and knows what to say in every situation. What was I thinking with my foolish crush on him? He's flashy, insincere, and nothing like Nikolay.

I'm envious that he doesn't have to hide all his feelings in situations, unlike Nikolay. He's been a part of our family since I was thirteen, coming from our hometown in Russia. I glance around to find him making the rounds with his "brothers" in what appears to be subdued conversations.

Mom calls for toasts. The room falls silent.

"To my dear husband. The man I loved; may he rest in peace."

The group chimes in with "hear, hear" before sipping their drinks. The toast rolls around the room and stops with me. I snag a glass of white wine off the table and lift it.

"To Papa." I hope it's sufficient and take a sip. What can I say about a man I didn't respect? Sure, he kept a roof over our heads, but there were no bedtime stories, and he never showed up at our school events. He was an absent father even though we lived in the same house. Someone else in the room toasts, and as others chime in, I sigh in relief that I didn't have to make a drawn-out speech.

"Well done," Nikolay whispers in my ear. His warm breath caresses my neck. My skin is peppered with bumps of … excitement? Anticipation? We're flirting with the inevitable. He knows it. I know it. I'm wondering what his plans are. We've not discussed much of anything. We keep to our rooms and only bump into each other in common areas and at dinner.

"Thank you." I'm ashamed I told him about caring for everyone when I lived here. It's not something we advertise in Russia. Women are expected to do what I did and more. Only it should have fallen to my mother.

I glance at my mom, who appears to be stronger than I remember. She was a wreck a few days ago, and now she pulls off the stature of a confident widow. I wonder why there's a sudden change in a woman who lived under Papa's iron fist. Could she have someone new? How can she so quickly transition past Papa's death after years of marriage?

"Your mother appears to be doing well," Nikolay comments. It appears he's noticed what I'm witnessing.

It's irritating how he reads my mind. Does he pick up on my body tensing with anticipation whenever he's near? Does he know I long for his touch? How well does he know me? I'm afraid to find out. He's a man who has enjoyed the bachelor life for years. In the Bratva, most men promise never to marry and live the playboy life-style and all that entails. And most mafia men have mistresses. Will he have one as well?

My sister has been busy online this week and sent me screenshots of Nikolay's yacht and articles about his nightlife here in London as the CEO of a huge hotel chain. I have no doubt women find him appealing. His aloof manner and indifference to everyone are new to me, but I prefer it to being ignored.

"Yes, I was thinking that myself. I'm tired. Can we leave?"

He takes the still-filled wine glass out of my hand and puts it on the table with his. "We're leaving," he announces, giving me a small smile.

"Thank you." I take in the room one last time as a single woman. On the way home, I text my sister from the Range Rover to tell her we left.

Home, funny how I've not been there long, yet it's become my sanc-tuary. I like Hazel. She's sweet, warm-hearted, older than my mother, and more enjoyable. It's nice to have an ally in the house, someone I can go to for advice and not be judged for it.

* * *

True to his word, Alex brings the Range Rover around to take me to school. I have no idea how he will blend in. My initial concerns about more murders have considerably subsided.

"I think this is unnecessary," I complain to Alex from the backseat. It seems I'm making myself stand out with all the fuss.

"I have my orders."

I stare at the back of his head, and seeing as how he's from a poor section of London, being my bodyguard and driver is a huge step up for him.

He parks. We get out, and I grab my backpack. I take a familiar path to a large lecture hall where the class is held.

"What are you going to do? Lurk?" I stare at him like he's an imposition.

"If that's what I need to do, yes."

"Will everyone know you're Mafia?"

"Don't know, don't care. Your father was murdered, and he was of considerable wealth. I don't find it hard to comprehend your need for protection. There are others here from dynasties who have security in the shadows; you just can't pick up on them as they blend in, having been trained well."

Good point. I hope he's right. Meanwhile, no one here knows it was my father who committed suicide, and I have to pretend it never happened, or I blow my cover.

I sit in the theater, and my friend, Darci, joins me.

"What's with the goon in the back?"

"Security, I suppose," I reply with no explanation, and she doesn't seem fazed.

"We are going out this Friday, are you joining us?"

Us, as in a small study group of men and women. I've clubbed with them before, and I hate to pass up an invite. I'm making up for lost time, seeing as I am getting married so quickly. My days of freedom are disappearing as we speak.

"I'll see if I can make it happen. Text me the details," I reply.

"Sure, it will be great, there is a new band playing at one of our places."

The lecture begins. I take notes and head to another building for another class when it's over. By afternoon my brain is in meltdown mode.

Alex is the largest man on campus, but in his defense, he isn't intrusive. We arrive home. My shoes echo as I walk over the floors. I head to the kitchen, and the house is quiet and appears empty. I don't see Nikolay or Pavel lurking in the hall. Hazel has a snack for me and mentions Nikolay is out.

I finish my cucumber sandwich and decide to investigate the other floors without a warden following me.

I head to the top floor to investigate the house further. I find it is filled with bedrooms, bathrooms, and a billiards room. Interesting. I head to the second floor and find the room I remember briefly from my first day, the one with a desk and bookcase. I enter, and the scent of Nikolay's cologne hangs in the air, he had to be here this morning.

The smell reminds me of my childhood, and I don't know where it comes from, but it's so familiar I could swear it's imprinted in my brain. I can't recall its association or meaning to me.

I run my hands over the books in the library. The British classics; Lady Chatterley's Lover and The Jungle Book, among others. They are bound in leather. I pick Little Women off the shelf, and for a minute, I'm taken back to grade school, remembering how I carried it around as a child. I loved Jo. Like me, she was the rebel who wanted to write and struggled for her dreams. I crack the book open and smell the ink on the pristine pages.

"What are you doing in here?"

I'm startled and clutch the book to my chest so I don't drop it before I turn to find Nikolay in the doorway. My heart skips a beat.

"I love books."

"Well, this is my office. You may read the books, only do it somewhere else."

"Fine."

He takes four long strides, and he's in front of me. I stand my ground. I remember how he wore his towel after swimming and remember the tattoos on his chest. I wonder what they mean. He's dangerous, but I know there must be another side to him. A side he won't show me.

"You're..." His words cut off as his lips descend on mine. They are warm and affectionate. I'm nervous as fuck, this is nothing like any kiss I've ever exchanged with any man. He leans over me, his hand above my head on the bookcase, his body pressing against mine as his other hand moves behind my back to keep me steady under the weight of him.

Wetness fills my panties. I can't deny the attraction we've been dancing around and kiss him back. His hand comes down and grabs my long hair, giving it a tug. The force of his movement causes my head to tilt back. He crushes my lips as I feverishly move my lips over his as his tongue thrusts into my mouth. I let him invade it, and the book slips from my hands as I wrap them around his neck. The kisses become increasingly demanding. His unexpected affection fuels my desire. His lips break away and travel down my neck, where he concentrates on one area, gently sucking before leaving a trail of kisses leading to the top of my blouse.

My instinct is to avoid the new sensations welling inside me. I want to squirm under the explosion of neurons firing. Everywhere he touches releases exquisite bursts of euphoria. I find myself wanting him, but I'm afraid to give in to him. He's used to getting what he wants. I can't let him in; it will make me weak, like Mum. I need to fight him if I'm to have my independence. Love makes women weak.

His body is pushing on me, and his hard cock presses against my abdomen.

Without reason, he breaks away.

"Another time, I have work to do." He turns away, regaining his composure, and says, "I heard you had classes today."

"Yes." My voice is unsteady. My lips are swollen. "Alex is nice." I should bring up the clubbing date, but I know he'll say no. I refuse to ask him for permission.

"You need to get on with the wedding planning."

"I'm working on it."

"Good." His dark blue eyes take me in. "Saturday morning," he announces out of the blue. "Don't forget."

Shopping with men. Ugh.

"Fine. Am I going alone?"

"No, I need to make sure your choices are appropriate. I doubt you'll know where to go."

The passive-aggressive behavior is wearing on me.

"I can figure out shopping. It's called Google."

He gives me a smirk. "Funny. And how are you to pay for designer dresses?"

"That's why you're going, I imagine," I sass him as I pick up the book and brush past him, making a perfect exit.

"Ten, be ready. Dinner tonight, usual time," I hear him say as I make my way into the hall.

"Got it."

After studying and texting Darci, I make my way downstairs as Mom and Kateryna arrive with Sergei.

I greet them at the door, and they are shocked as soon as they enter the grand foyer.

"Have you gotten lost in the house?" Kateryna asks as she waltzes into the foyer. "Does it echo?"

She's out of school, so the wedding planning comes at a good time.

"I don't know," I reply as she peers up at the staircase.

"My goodness, this is amazing," Mom gushes.

"Thanks. Let's go into the living room. Hazel made scones, and we'll have tea." I nod to Sergei, who wears a smirk. I wonder what that's about. He's turned into an arrogant jerk since Papa died.

We spent an hour planning the wedding, the flowers, the cake, nothing too elaborate. My sister has the list of guests Nikolai delivered to her via Sergei. The invitations will be hand-delivered by courier due to the short notice and needed privacy.

"There aren't many people," Mom says.

"It's fine. I don't want a large group." In my mind, I don't want to be different from my friends, who profess never to marry or have kids. Besides, my life mate has been decided for me. Ergo, no option.

"Oh, did you hear the sad news on Baran?"

"No, what?"

"He was found dead in his apartment shortly after Papa was found. We were questioned," Katerynia continues.

"No, no one told me. I never imagined. I thought it strange he wasn't around the day of Papa's…"

"Right, strange, huh?" My sister has a point. I involuntarily shiver even though the room isn't cold. Nikolay dispatched Pavel to make sure he paid for Papa's untimely end. Did Nikolay's order do this?

"Don't dwell on it, girls," Mum intercedes with the sad news. "We must be going. I'll write out the invitations. You need to pick your menu items for the dinner after the ceremony."

"Fine," I concede. It's not so bad doing this with help. It's not what I dreamed about, but then again, Baran's death reminds me of why I'm agreeing to this antiquated ritual of marrying for wealth or power. In my case, it's both.

Dinnertime comes, so I slip into a nicer dress, knowing Nikolay likes to keep dinner formal. Tonight, he surprises me by showing up in jeans. I'm confused.

"I thought dinner had a dress code."

"I didn't have time to change." His nonchalant reply surprises me. He pulls my chair out, and I sit, tucking my dress like a lady.

Hazel arrives with our dinner plates. I admire her smooth serving skills and how professional she is when it's evident she cares for the family. She tends the house like it's her own. All day she cleans and cooks and always has snacks for anyone, no matter what time of day it is.

"I see you planned dinner," he muses as his hamburger and fries sit under his nose.

"Not any burger, these are made with the best meat, you'll love it. Dip your fries in the aioli sauce with truffles."

He shakes his head as if in disbelief that a burger is his dinner.

"I thought I could pick food," I explain.

"It's fine," he concedes as he dips a fry into the sauce. I watch as he chews and swallows. "It's good."

Why am I working so hard to please him? He's said nothing of the kisses in his office. My back is sore from getting crushed against the bookcase, but I kinda like the reminder.

Secretly, I long to feel him again. He left me so horny I didn't know what to do. However, I managed to get myself off with my vibrator, and as I orgasm, his face is in my mind.

<h1 style="text-align:center">CHAPTER 7</h1>

NIKOLAY

As much as I wanted to fuck her, I didn't want Anya's first time to be up against the library doors. Luckily for me, my better judgment won out. I must be going soft because it never mattered before. Anya drives me crazy, at times trying to please me and at others, testing the limits of my patience.

The wedding is being planned, and Anya asks for her sister to join her when shopping for her wedding dress. With Alex taking them, I don't care as long as she's safe. The stores are filled with men waiting on wives and girlfriends. They might as well be sitting on death row, time wasted, and boring as fuck. Today, she has classes, and I suspect she'll work on the details of our small wedding.

I need to shop for a ring befitting a young bride. Anya is stunning, and her vibrant blue eyes are the last thing I see before I fall asleep at night. I can't deny her status within the Bratva; she will be the one to bear my children even if I'm not ready for it. Thankfully, she probably wants to finish school first.

I visit a famous jewelry store and find a sapphire surrounded by diamonds set in white gold.

"She'll love it." I hand it back to the salesman.

Pavel chuckles. "Sure, just a young schoolgirl. How many dollars are you spending?"

I'm convinced the ring will impress her. She has her nose in all those glamour magazines for a reason. My little bird is fascinated by glamorous lifestyles and fashion. She has exquisite taste in the few expensive items she owns, and I have no doubt she'd love to emulate women who set the bar on fashion trends. I can't wait to take her on a honeymoon and show her the world's best restaurants.

I smile as the clerk puts the light blue box in the monogrammed bag.

"Statements are important, I don't have to tell you. The image of her in that brief business attire, marching off to her classes, sends a rush of desire through me. She'll be mine before the wedding. She'll be mine before the wedding bells chime.

Pavel lets out a low whistle and chides me. "I'm surprised it's taken you this long." He's the only one who can tease me like this. The ride home is an opportunity to work, so Pavel drives, and I use the back seat as a portable office. Fires to put out, meetings to arrange, it's endless.

I'm elated to see Alex's SUV parked in the driveway when I arrive. I'm looking forward to seeing Anya, and dinner is a neutral ground in which we can converse without every sentence igniting her rebellion.

I had a long day going through information with Konstantin and Pavel. My brain is fried, overwhelmed by the numerous rackets Igor had set up and even participated in with other smaller criminal organizations. Pavel researched Anya's father, and it appears the oil company executives may have made remarks that were not favorable to Russia's leadership. Similarly, others from the oil giant have been found murdered while vacationing. One fell overboard while in the Mediterranean on a yacht. Another jumped off a high-rise in France. Of course, they were all ruled as suicides.

This is why my father never got involved with large organizations where anyone can shoot their mouth off and think there will be no repercussions, so I wonder how this debacle took his life. Dad liked to be in control of his own destiny and always shielded his identity from the lower rungs of the Bratva. His old-school way of doing things gave us decades of protection without losing top leaders. Unlike Italian mobsters in the States, where everyone has dirt on someone, we've compartmentalized. Our lowest-ranking soldiers can't give us up to avoid prison time. Russians are tough. Prison means another tattoo and is worn with honor. Most bravely fall on their sword to protect the Bratva.

I pull the ring box out of the bag and place it on my dresser before I shower and change into casual clothing for dinner. I've decided to lighten up on the formal dining as we'll entertain more after Anya graduates. She has enough on her plate with wedding preparations. I shouldn't care about her so much, but she's more relaxed and talkative when she's not forced to do my bidding. This is a small compromise with no consequences. I tug my fitted jeans on, pull a polo over my head, and spritz cologne before I step into leather loafers. I can't deny I look forward to dinnertime.

Anya is already there and talking to Hazel when I arrive. I didn't expect her to be here so early.

"How was your day?" I ask as Anya sits. I slide her chair in before I pour from the bottle of expensive red wine sitting on the table. I take note of the fact she has discovered the wine cellar.

"Great, classes went well, and Mum and Katerynia are working on the wedding. I'm going along with this marriage to protect my family. I want my sister to marry for love. So, don't get the impression I'm doing any of this for you."

"Agreed, I never wanted to marry someone young and inexperienced, so we're on the same page," I agree. It's easier to placate her and end the argument.

"We're having French food tonight," she announces as she places her napkin in her lap.

The flowers on the table have been replaced with fresh Gerbera daisies. Clearly, Anya likes making decisions.

I use my knife to push aside the fresh green beans I cut. They will go perfectly with the steak. I take a credit card out of my pocket and slide it to her. "For anything you need. Enjoy shopping. We'll change the name on it after the wedding."

She nods and slides the card to the other side of her plate. I'm sure she knows there's no limit to the amount she can spend, judging by the company name it bears and the fact it's a black card.

"This weekend is reserved for getting you fitted properly," I add.

"It will be cutting it close. Mom is sending out the invitations to your requested dinner. It's in the afternoon, followed by an outdoor seated dinner under tents. There will be lights for dancing, so I ordered a wood dance floor that will be laid over the grass."

"No, it will kill the grass. Do you know how much that costs? Replacing grass is a bitch," I grumble before taking another bite of steak.

She raises her eyebrows. "I'm sure you can afford it with the size of this place. Let's not forget we have to paint the perfect picture to sell this. And you need me to do that." She smirks.

Damn. She's got a point. At times, she has me over a barrel. I need her to pave my way into combining the Bratvas, and even though she can't lead it, her name has clout. It also brings fear, as her father was a target. Two men have died, and I'm told the underbosses are getting jumpy.

I can't afford to add more discord. I lean back in my chair and chew the flavorful meat. I never guessed Anya would know international cuisine. She's full of surprises for someone who lived a sheltered life. I need to stop worrying about the wedding. Providing a happy occasion to lift the heavy dread infiltrating our nostrils will be worth the price of every dollar this wedding will cost. It's what the men need, what we all need. Anya's been a good diversion to keep my mind off my own father's untimely demise. I think of him often when I have decisions to make and wonder what he would do in the same situation.

A night off for my top men will get them to relax and let them see another side of me, the one I am when I'm not ordering men around like a tyrant, even though it's good for the business.

I also need to meet with some unsavory men of my own to keep the drugs and weapons flowing in and out. In addition, there are the hotels, sex clubs, and bars we own. Each brings their own challenges. I can no longer split my time between Russia and the US. Our organization requires a full-time leader with clout. I'm sure we'll figure something out in time.

Anya asked me a question about accommodations. I told her my two brothers and mother will fly in for the affair. Mama will stay with us, and my brothers will remain at another estate we own. We have enough money, we could all live in London, or anywhere for that matter.

"Are we getting an official honeymoon? Or are we having a staycation?"

"I need a break, I thought we'd take my yacht and travel somewhere warm. Would you like that?"

"That would be nice. I have a passport."

"I thought the French Riviera would be nice." I take a sip of the wine and let it settle on my palate.

"Really? That would be great. My classes end soon and won't resume until fall."

"Perfect, are you a fan of the water?"

"I haven't been to a beach in years, but I think I'll like it." She demurely sips the lovely red wine the color of her lips. She closes her eyes to enjoy the flavor. It's as if she's taunting me to seduce her.

I have a mind to lean over and taste the wine lingering in her mouth, and as I'm leaning forward to make my move, the doorbell rings. Who could be here on a Friday night?

"That must be my sister." Anya leaps to her feet, wipes her mouth, and dashes to the open door. Alex is off for the night, so it's a different guard answering the door. Anya stays in after dinner. This has been her routine as she doesn't have night classes.

I follow her so I can greet my future sister-in-law.

"Kateryna." I kiss both her cheeks. "What brings you out tonight?"

"I wanted to see my sister, and we have wedding things to go over," she replies as she clutches magazines with brides on them to her chest.

"Let me take your coat," I offer.

"Thank you."

She slides out of a cheaply made discount jacket. I'm appalled Igor kept his family on a tight budget. It's so... unoriginal. When his bank accounts are in order, the women in the family will have enough money to meet their needs and then some. Things are tied up now, but I suspect they will be released soon. Money talks louder than words.

"We're going upstairs," Anya announces before Kateryna gives me a tiny wave, then they race up the steps, giggling the whole way.

It's times like this I'm reminded how young my fiancée is. The upside is she's still capable of conforming to lifestyle changes and new rules. I can't help but curl my lips into a smirk; it will be fun breaking her in.

I retire to my living room on the second floor, poring over my encrypted laptop with contracts I need to read. We have solicitors, but I trust no one.

CHAPTER 8

ANYA

*D*inner offers us a space where a truce exists. I enjoy perusing the fine wines from the cellar and selecting vintages to go with our dinners. I love looking up new things for Hazel to cook. Eating is like traveling the world without the price tag. I'm not used to having someone cook for me, but Hazel isn't complaining about the new challenges I've thrown her. In our many conversations, she told me she went to a school to be a chef and doesn't mind serving us. The house was previously on low staff and sat empty most of the time. We'll need more people to run the mansion at some point.

Nikolay's cologne arrives with him and stirs memories of my past. I was young, very young, but I can't place it. It's irritating as hell. It doesn't conjure bad memories, just memories I can't recall.

"Nikolay, how was your day?" I play the dutiful wife. This is the type of home life I want. A man home for dinner, a home I never imagined, and staff to wait on me. I should pinch myself to make sure it's not a dream.

"Busy, as usual," he replies as if we've known each other forever. I'll probably never know what he does when calls come late at night, and he has to rush out. His role as the King is new to both of us. I, however, had no time to prepare for it. He fills our glasses. Hazel brings the food, and our dinner ritual starts. I never dreamed I would love sitting in the same room with him when we met. He's easy on the eyes, but his gruff, abrupt retorts have me second-guessing myself. I can't deny the attraction between us, and it's driving me crazy. I need to hate him, but I want him.

I control my enthusiasm over the honeymoon. If I let him know what I like, he might use it to punish me for not conforming to his every whim. He doesn't need to know I've been dying to use my passport to go anywhere but Russia!

I learned a few tactics from Papa. He was savvy at chess and poker; I never could read him, so I lost every game we played. I prefer games where one wins by skill, not craft, like soccer. Not that I've played much. I like the challenge of school and earning the grades I get. I take pride in accomplishing my goals.

Dinner is over, and Kateryna arrives as planned. After greetings, we're left to our own devices. If only Nikolay knew how dangerous it is leaving the two of us without supervision.

"Kat, thanks for coming!" We kick off our shoes and dive onto my huge bed.

"Oh, I miss hearing from you. You're too busy, and you aren't even married," she exclaims as she picks up a pillow and beats me with it. I pick up the other one and hit her back, and we're laughing. It's nice to break up the reality of this being the first time we're alone together since Papa died.

"I'm here; you need to text more. How are you, really?" I ask.

"Sad, but each day I'm better. Mum is doing better than expected."

"No wonder there. She's young enough to get her own life," I add.

"Anya! We were her life." She clutches the pillow to her chest as she sits. She crosses her legs and faces me.

"I just mean she doesn't have to live how Papa wanted her to."

"It must be scary; I'm worried about college. Mom said she can pay for it, but I don't know what I want to do."

"It will come to you. The experience will be good for you."

We both fall onto our backs and lie with our heads on the pillow like old times. We're close in age and, as such, we share many interests. She's just now leaving her formal schooling and is on her tenth crush. She was afraid to disagree with Papa and lived a life where she kept her friends hidden.

Sergei was the keeper of our secrets. He never sold us out if we were up past bedtime texting friends or talking on the phone, even if we were grounded. However, he kept the security cameras working, much to my dismay.

I know we have cameras here, but I doubt there are any in my bedroom.

"How are the wedding plans coming?" I ask to cover the bases.

"Fine. Don't worry. We have ice sculptures and a photo booth. This house is large enough to accommodate everyone—with how many bathrooms? Six?"

"Something like that," I agree.

"We're shopping tomorrow morning, right?"

"Oh, yes, I need to find a wedding dress, and Nikolay gave me a credit card. We can spend whatever we want."

Kat giggles. "Papa would never do that."

"Is the will being settled? The tabloids are reporting he was worth a ton of money." I love to follow breaking news. I never dreamed we'd be the news.

"Probably. Why?"

"Well, you can marry anyone you want and leave this world behind."

Her pretty lips frown. "Why would I want to leave you?"

"Not me, but the life; you can go to another country, or city where no one knows who you are. You can marry for love and get out of the family with a life of crime. Can you imagine going to school with Papa's suicide following you? You could get a new identity. What if someone marries you for your money? What if the bad guys are after us?"

"I never thought of it."

"I'm marrying Nikolay so you can be free to do what you want," I explain. "He's our protection. You can marry whomever you want, but I want you to get a career first."

"But what about you?"

"I'm fine. I'm strong enough to stand up to him or any man who wants to bully me."

"That you are," she agrees, no doubt she's remembering the fight with Papa over school. "I feel guilty you can't marry for love."

"It's what a big sister is for, to protect you. I can take care of myself. Don't worry about me. Promise me you won't marry a douchebag."

"I'll try my best. Most men are fickle. Tell me, how are your studies going?"

"Good, perfect timing for all this wedding stuff."

"Are you nervous about, y'know?"

"It won't be much. For all I know, he has a woman on the side already."

"Anya! That's not right."

"Things were never 'right' with Papa being a part of the mafia, either."

"True. So, what do you need me to do tonight? Your text was cryptic; I am relieved to see you and to see you are okay." She rolls on her side and perches her head on her palm. I roll to face her.

"I have a date with my friend Darci. We're going to a club."

"Does Nikolay know? I'm sure he won't be happy."

"He doesn't have to know. I figure it's my chance to get out one last time. I'm sure it's not the 'Bratva' way. I swear it's like Yoda speaking a secret every time he says 'Bratva.'"

Kat snickers, and it's refreshing, as Papa had a dry sense of humor.

My phone beeps: Darci, she wants me to meet her at a hip new club in London.

"Can I wear your jacket and use your car? I can get past the cameras if I pose as you. I think…"

"What? What am I to do while you're gone?"

"Wait here. I'll be fine. I'll be home by one, and we'll switch back. The clubs aren't busy until eleven anyway. No one will know. It's like old times."

"Won't you get in trouble? What if someone is after you?"

"Doubtful. I'm not important. No one at school knows me. If anything, they're more likely to be after Konstantin or Nikolay; they hold the organization together." I sit up and hug my sister. "Please, I need to get out," I plead with my Kat.

"What if you get hurt?" She stands. "What am I to do?"

"There's a flat-screen TV on the wall. Just stay in here and text me if there are any problems."

I stand, and she joins me. I take her hands in mine. "Through thick and thin."

"Thick and thin, but if your bloody fiancé finds out, I'm not to blame. I don't want to be on his shit list." She follows me to the powder room as I use a brush and apply makeup. Kat's hair is in a messy bun. I quickly flip mine to look like hers. It takes ten minutes before I hug her and assure her everything will be like old times.

"We haven't done this in ages," Kat adds excitedly as she moves behind me at the vanity in the bathroom and plays with my hair.

"Shit." She looks around the huge bathroom. "You have a tub and a shower. Man, this is so cool."

"I know, right?" I glance at her reflection in the mirror as she checks out my walk-in closet, which has the clothes Nikolay had pre-arranged to be here when I arrived. It's a sweet collection of expensive shoes, and then there is the tiny corner where my clothes live; three dresses, a business suit in pink and black, and a spring coat.

"Where did the nice stuff come from?"

"Nikolay. I have no idea how he accomplished it, but it's awesome, don't you think?"

"Of course." She stands enamored with what is the basis of what will become my new wardrobe.

"We'll get you cool new stuff, too," I explain.

"So, has he... done the deed?"

"What? No!"

"Well, I can tell he likes you. Why else would he even care to say 'hi' to me? And your closet makes a statement. It's not cheap, Anya."

"I know. He's sociable, but he's very keen on keeping things between us businesslike."

"How would you know if he has a woman on the side? I don't doubt plenty of women are willing to sleep with a married man."

"I don't know. I've never had a serious relationship before. It's not that I haven't wondered about it myself. What if he does cheat? Is that why he hasn't come into my room at night? There's nothing stopping him from doing what he wants. Does he not like me?"

"Well, maybe he's waiting for the wedding. You haven't been with anyone, have you?" She fiddles with my brushes on the counter.

"No, heavens, I wish. No one is special for me. You?"

"No one here, small crushes. I take my time."

I've always viewed my sister as the normal one. She's great at small talk, fits into any situation, views slights as just words, and takes nothing personally. She doesn't waste time on situations that don't matter in the long run. I'm envious of how she sails through life with little stress.

"Thank you for this, Kat. I owe you." I peer into the mirror to see her face above mine as I sit in a padded chair designed for the table.

"You'll owe me a ton if you get caught, so be home on time and text me you are on your way home so I don't worry. I can't believe we're doing this. We haven't played twins in years," she replies. As much as she wants to be the heavy, she smiles.

"It will be fine," I assure her. "This isn't our first time breaking rules."

"Yeah, but Sergei had our back."

"True, we'll just have to wing it. I'm sure it will be fine. Make yourself at home, and don't leave the room. No one comes in here anyway."

I dress in jeans like my sister's and wear her blouse. I stuff a Lycra mini dress in my purse. I plan to change it before we meet at the club. I turn the TV on, and it's as if my sister and I have fallen back in time when we were best friends living under one roof.

At nine, I check the hallway and decide to make a break for it before Nikolay goes to bed, usually after ten. He's an early riser. I keep my head down, descend the stairs, and grab my sister's jacket from a small closet in the foyer. I'm confident I haven't lost my touch and waltz out the door to her car. I find it funny I'm acting like Cinderella being whisked off to a ball, but we want the same thing—freedom for a night to mingle with peers.

With her purse over my shoulder and her car keys safely in my hand, I wave goodnight to the guard on the grounds and crawl into my sister's old, yellow VW Bug. The guards on the grounds will never suspect a thing.

God, this thing is ancient and small. I've become accustomed to being chauffeured around and feel like I'm in a time warp. I push the clutch in and crank the car. I take the emergency brake off and the car putters. I'm off, out the gates, and driving towards freedom. It's been a week since I've had a minute to myself outside our estate.

I park and change in the car, which is difficult considering the fact there are two seats and the gearshift. I pull my purse out, lock the car, and join Darci in the queue. I left the jacket in the car; the night air is chilly, and I rub my arms to stay warm.

"Oh my God," Darci exclaims as she hugs me. "You made it!"

"I did."

People behind us in the queue gripe over me jumping the line.

"Piss off," Darci exclaims. I know she'll make a good attorney. She's not intimidated by anyone.

"I saw in the paper your dad was murdered. Sorry about that?"

"Really?" Nikolay didn't say anything about it.

"Oh, yes, a picture of you and a man named Nikolay, Russian, eh? You were in the tabloids leaving your house. I recognized you."

Really? I'm aghast I missed this pertinent information. I assume she's referring to the pictures the media took of us after we left my flat. I hope she'll let it go. I guess the cat is out of the bag now.

"I'm sorry about your dad. Weird stuff going on," she adds without asking questions, for which I'm grateful. But then it occurs to me that she seems to know the behind-the-scenes details that no one would know outside of our inner circle. What does she mean by weird stuff? What does she know that she's not sharing?

"Sure is," I reply. "I try not to think about it. My father wasn't the best dad in the world." I shrug.

"Your fiancé is a looker. Good for you." She nudges me, and I smile.

He is a looker, and his aloof nature is driving me crazy. I can't stop thinking about him; his cold, translucent eyes remind me of frozen lakes in the Russian countryside.

The line moves, and we show our IDs and pay to enter the newest club. The music is loud, making talking impossible.

Darci motions towards the bar. I follow right behind her as she cuts a path through the crowd of young people. New clubs are always packed, and tonight is no exception. The circular bar has neon blue lighting underneath it. There's an upper level with a railing for guests to lean on and a good place if one wants to check out the hotties below.

"Two martinis," she yells to the handsome bartender.

A minute later she turns and hands me a drink. I take a sip.

"Blimey, this is strong!"

"It's supposed to be. At fifteen dollars a drink, it better be strong."

It sounds like highway robbery, but I'm buzzed after a few sips. We circulate around the dance floor and watch the crowd jump around to the beat of techno music.

Darci finds classmates, and we join them in a less noisy corner of the room where we catch up. I don't know them well. I suck at group social skills, preferring one-on-one conversations with meaning, so I listen. I thought this would be fun, even exhilarating, but I find myself missing the comforts of home, knowing Nikolay is just down the hall. I wonder when he'll make the move we've been dancing around all week.

I look over my shoulder to make sure we're not being followed and put my empty glass on a table. As a group, we decide to hit the dance floor. I allow myself to get caught up in the music, and the room begins to spin. I tell myself it will wear off. It's not like I haven't been drunk before, but that drink had a kick to it.

I'm wondering how Darci knew it was me in the paper. Sure, there was a picture with a telephoto lens. I doubt it would be clear enough for her to piece it together. Who would even be thinking a school chum would be someone in the news with a different name? It's a lot to piece together. I've never shared much about my life, my sister and mom, sure, but nothing would give away my real name. Papa insisted I use a different name in school for safety. She knows my secret, yet she hasn't questioned me on the reason behind it, and with that thought, the room blurs. I know I'm in trouble.

I stumble away from the group and clutch a tabletop. The patrons give me a 'fuck off' look. I think I'm going to be sick.

Just as I'm about to pass out, strong hands grab me.

CHAPTER 9

NIKOLAY

I'm sipping cognac when Mother calls.

"Mama, how are you?"

"I try to move forward. The good days mix with moments in which I'm out of tears. It comes in waves. I miss your father. How is it going there? I haven't heard from you. I wanted to make sure you were okay. I hate sending you there to clean up this mess. I'm happy you're getting married. It's time you took a wife. We need new blood in the family. Kids bring energy into the house."

This must be the next phase after the grieving. She's looking forward to activities to motivate her to get out of bed every day. It's been under two weeks since she lost her husband, so she's doing well. After thirty-five years of marriage, she deserves as much time as she needs. His death left a gaping hole in her heart and everyday life. Grandchildren will fill her life, but I foresee our life rotating in and out of Russia. Eventually, I'll have a brother take over Russia; it makes sense to conquer and divide. If I can't trust my brothers, I'm really fucked.

"I'll do my best, Mama. Anya loves London." I lean back in my chair, and her comforting voice soothes me. She is a good mother. My instincts tell me Anya will be too, especially after I hear snippets of her father, who was a piece of work.

"Don't get carried away. Anya and I are still strangers. We were kids when we last met. I'll give you grandkids, just not now. I have a job to do." All the while I really have no idea what Anya thinks. I've never discussed it with her because it's a foregone conclusion.

"Don't forsake the good things in life. You can be too serious at times. I think Anya will be good for you. You need to be married before you become too set in your ways. It's harder to change and compromise the older you get. I'm pissed at Igor. He was never good with the politics of our world, or elected officials. Your father warned him to avoid oil companies, but somehow, he ultimately landed out of favor." She sighs. "He wasn't fastidious with details like you. I wonder what Dmitry will find. We may never know why either of them were killed. How is Anya? I haven't seen her in ages."

"She's well. However, she hasn't mentioned us. I don't think she remembers our time in Russia. She was young," I add. I'm shocked because she never mentioned her over the years. Maybe she thought it was only a crush between us. Maybe she didn't know of our attraction. We fit together so well even then.

"Sure, I was friends with her mother, and we did things together. Then we moved to the city, and they went to London. It was part of the plan to divide and conquer." She lets out a long sigh as if she's exhausted by reminiscing over the past.

"I remember Anya, but I didn't think you would. She was a cute kid." I reflect on memories I buried years ago, yet they return to me like yesterday.

"Yes, she was. But you loved to tease her. You would pull her pigtails and give her flowers you picked from the vacant fields. They smelled of mint and sage."

I sink back into the sofa, taking a large sip of my liquor. I daydream about the small town where we were born, like the flowers growing by the dirt roads we walked. Anya always had her nose in a book. The kids made fun of her because she'd rather read than play ball in the schoolyard. She loved Little Women. I assume it's because it was because it presented an alternate reality for her. Nothing exciting ever happened in our neighborhood. Most dads spent their weekly paycheck buying vodka in the local bars and fought with their wives when they made it home.

Sure, I teased her. Kids do tease each other. It means nothing. I remember leaving a note inside her book asking her to meet me on the playground to walk her home, and she'd tell me about the novels she was reading. Some, like "Little Women," were not legal. I now recall how she clutched it to her chest in my office with the library. She made me promise to keep it a secret. My little Anya is all grown up. A grin forms on my tired face. This would explain the chemistry between us, I'm sure of it. As children and adults, we gravitated toward each other; it turned into a burning flame. She's never far from my thoughts. I pushed her to the back of my mind over the years, thinking it was fate telling me we were not to be when they suddenly moved away. I was sure our parents were conspiring against me and us.

"I doubt she remembers any of it. She was so young at the time," Mama adds wistfully. "How are the wedding plans coming along?"

"Anya and her family are taking care of it." I sigh and pour more cognac from the crystal bottle sitting in front of me. I never thought about living away from home permanently. I used to come to London to oversee things for Dad but could return home when I wanted. Now, I'm grounded here. I miss Mama, having taken her for granted as I grew older. I miss my nightlife at the clubs. Keeping track of Anya in uncertain times requires time and energy when I'm trying to manage a merger of our family's businesses.

"How are Dmitry and Roman?" I ask. I miss them giving me shit all the time.

"Trouble, as always." She sighs, and I'm sure she remembers us when we were younger. "I miss your presence; you tend to keep them in line the best."

I chuckle. "Well, I'll be seeing you next week."

"That you will. I'll bring pearls for Anya to wear at the wedding and welcome her to the family. How are you two getting along?"

"Fine."

"She must love the house. She always had her head in the clouds. I'm surprised she wants to be an attorney."

"You know?"

"Of course, it's good for you to be with a woman who won't give in to your every demand. It will keep you on your toes."

"Sure, one more person for me to keep in line."

"It's late. I have to go. I'll see you next week." She tells me she loves me and hangs up.

I ponder our conversation. I wonder if Anya has memories of her childhood in Russia. The small town where our fathers grew up is all she knows outside of London. This explains why she's so modern and adventuresome. She's more European than Russian. She's had freedoms most from our town never experienced.

It's past my bedtime when my phone rings. It's Pavel.

"What now? It's late."

"I got a call. Anya is at Club Royal. Our doorman texted as they went in. Some girl was with her."

"Her sister?"

"Hell, if I know. Doubtful, dark-haired. Anya and Katerynia are both blonde."

"How did she get out of the house? Fuck!" I exclaim. "I'll check her room. Pick me up immediately."

I fly up the steps, taking two at a time, and burst through Anya's bedroom door to find Katerynia in her bed, eating a candy bar and watching TV. Her eyes grow wide with surprise.

"Where is Anya?"

"At a club with a classmate."

"When did she leave?"

"Over an hour ago. I'm sorry." She stands. "Wait, how did you know? No one came by the room. Is she okay?"

"I don't know. She's on her own, at night, with no guard. You tell me," I yell in frustration. "I'm going to get her. You stay here and don't leave this room!"

Katerynia shrinks under my voice. I slam the door behind me so hard it rattles the frame.

I grab a suit jacket from my room and exit the front door as Pavel pulls up in our black SUV.

"Fuck, do we have any intel on who she's with?"

"No, the staff is looking for her as we speak."

"Fuck, fuck, fuck!" I strike the dashboard as Pavel floors it to our club.

Pavel parks illegally on the street, and we hop out, charging into the club as if our lives depended on it. My heart is in my throat. What if something happened to her? Who is she here with? Is she secretly meeting a man?

I dismiss the last thought. She's not the type to cheat. She's a straight arrow, except for tonight. I don't like being played, not by a rival and definitely not by my fiancée.

Pavel receives a text instructing us to go to the back of the club. I see her first, bent over a table. I would be filled with relief if I weren't so angry.

I place my arm on hers, scaring the patrons at the table. Obviously, they aren't with her. "Look for her friend," I yell with a malevolent voice.

Anya's eyes are glassy, and she's slow to react.

"The girl hasn't been found. The men are on it."

"We need to get her home. She's been drugged." I sweep Anya into my arms, worried about her health, but assume it was a club drug that will make her woozy, and the effects intensify with alcohol. I have a doctor on call if needed. I don't want an inquiry into our new club.

"How much did you drink?"

Her head is limp in my arm, "Little, little, tiny…" her voice trails off.

I'm in panic mode even though I need to be calm. I've never been responsible for a woman before, and it's gut-wrenching worrying about what she was given and who meant to harm her. I'll slice and dice any man who puts a hand on her.

Pavel opens the back door of our vehicle, and I place Anya inside, run to the other side, and crawl in next to her. I click her seatbelt around her even though I'm holding her to my chest tightly. As a precaution, I keep her head upright.

"I feel so…sick," she murmurs weakly, laying her head on my shoulder.

"What did you drink?"

"Martini." Saliva is seeping out of her mouth as if it's numb. "I'm thirsty." Her words are mumbled as if she's high, slow to process, and limited.

"We'll be home soon. Keep talking. Who did you meet tonight?"

"Dar…ci."

"Is she from school?"

"Um."

"Stay awake. I need to make sure you're breathing."

"I'm tired. I want to sleep."

"I know."

"Is she okay, boss?" Pavel checks on us from the rearview mirror, concern on his face.

"So far, call the doctor to meet us at the house. I suspect it is Rohypnol. It should wear off in a few hours. But we need to make sure. She might need an antidote."

Anya is the key to bringing the Petrov and Volkov Bratva together. Our merger will accomplish what our fathers always desired, a large-scale underworld organization between them, working together and growing their business into a worldwide enterprise.

"Right." Pavel calls our personal doctor on Bluetooth, and fifteen minutes later, we're home.

"Oh, my God, is she okay?" Kateryna flies down the stairs upon our arrival. No doubt the doors crashing open could be heard upstairs.

"Hopefully," I reply with a menacing glance. "Pavel, have the house guard take her home."

"Yes, sir."

"Is she okay?" Kateryna yells again as she comes to her sister's side.

"She will be. And if you ever play games like this again, there will be hell to pay!"

"I'm sorry, she wanted to go out," she replies as Pavel grabs her arms and escorts her back to Anya's room. She gathers her belongings, and he turns her over to another guard in the house to drive her home.

I carry Anya to my massive suite, throw the covers on my bed back with a flick of my wrists, and lay her on the soft mattress. Her red minidress leaves little to the imagination, and there is no way she's wearing skimpy clothing like that for anyone but me.

Hazel appears with cold water in a glass. I force her to drink. She sips slowly. My heart breaks seeing her frail and weak. She's incapacitated. Thank God we got there in time. I'm not accustomed to seeing her helpless, and I wish I could do more.

I pray to myself she'll be fine and hope she lives so she can banter and sass me until my dying day. I pull over a chair to sit by her side. She drifts in and out.

Pavel arrives in the doorway. "How is she?"

"Drinking, it's a good sign. It could be Ecstasy. We have to cover the bases."

"Doc's on his way," Pavel relays with an urgency in his voice. No doubt we're all operating on adrenaline. An attack on Anya is an attack on us.

"She uses a fake name at school. Who would have known who she is?"

"Girls talk. It could be anyone. My instinct tells me this Darci is in the wind."

Hazel's voice can be heard in the hallway, and the doctor is with her.

"Doctor." I shake his hand. "Thank you for coming."

"I heard of the incident. I'll take blood. We'll test for drugs. How is she?"

"I'm keeping her awake, and she's sipping water."

He nods, then proceeds to the bed, where he administers an antidote and draws blood.

"I think she'll be okay. The antidote may be overkill, given her symptoms. I doubt they wanted to kill her."

"Why do you say that?"

"Chances are she was to be taken. By whom? That's for you to figure out. Overdoses usually happen to heavy drug users. Again, it's just my opinion."

I thank him, and he tells me to call if she's not improving. Other than that, we need time. Hazel sees him out.

Pavel is on the phone and hangs up.

"No sign of this Darci, and if she was in her class, I assume she, too, had a fake name. I think we need to look into the people who knew Anya's fake name."

"Agreed. We'll start that tomorrow. We were in the news with pictures. She might have put it together, but then again, she might be a plant. For now, I can't focus on anything other than getting recovering. I won't rest until I know she's over the worst of this drug."

Pavel nods and talks to the crew still looking for the mysterious Darci. Our soldiers will be looking over security footage at the club.

I sit in a chair by the bed and hold Anya's hand.

"You could have died. That's not part of the bargain, my dear." I doubt she can hear me. "When we were kids, I promised to marry you, and I won't be shortchanged."

CHAPTER 10

ANYA

I wake to find Nikolay in a chair by the bed, rubbing his elegant hand over the scruff on his powerful jaw. His eyes have dark circles under them. Judging from last night's clothes, he's been here all night.

I squirm and realize I can move, an improvement from last night when I was paralyzed.

"What happened?" I prop myself up in bed, and Nikolay rushes to put pillows behind me.

"You were drugged, but you're fine. Thankfully, our man at the door alerted us to the fact you were there. Otherwise..." He shakes his head and shrugs as if the alternative would have been a disaster.

"Who drugged me?" I'm alert at last. I scoot my butt to sit higher; thankfully, he leaned over to put pillows behind my back. I'm sure I look like a wreck, and it's the last thing I want to hear. "Darci?" I ask, the fog lifting from my memory.

"We assume Darci. Your sister knew her name." He stands and paces. "She's in the wind." He rubs his hand over the more than five o'clock shadow on his face.

"I thought it was strange, the way she was talking last night. She seemed to know a lot about me. She recognized me from the picture the media obtained outside my flat. Who does that? I mean, who would put two and two together that quickly?"

"Really? Interesting." He paces and contemplates before asking, "Any details worth sharing?"

"No, she was overly familiar, saying things she would never have known. She insisted on buying me a drink. After I drank the martini, I started to feel sick. I thought she was my friend. I never dreamed she would drug me."

"One never does. It happens so often and is easily accomplished. The bartender is being questioned."

"She knew who you were?" He continues to pace and think out loud as the sexual tension builds between us. I'm in his bed, wearing his large, monogrammed, long-sleeved shirt to keep the draft off my shoulders. I'm embarrassed he must have seen me naked unless he tasked Hazel to change me out of my skimpy dress. No, the outfit is befitting of a single girl who likes clubbing. I have no doubt he wouldn't want anyone he knows to see me in it. He'd probably chastise me for being too young again. On the other hand, maybe it's his possessive demeanor taking over.

I don't know why he didn't walk to my room and get my clothes. I touch the fabric bunched up over my hips; the heavy fabric is an exquisite weave. I love how it feels on my naked body. I love it more because it's been on his chest and is an extension of him. It's as if he's saying I'm his, and he's sharing one of his most intimate possessions with me.

"I mean, she knew I came from money and where I lived. But last night, she knew my real name, which confused me. I never told her."

"This is why we have rules. I have to assume an enemy of your father's or someone who wants to unseat me will go after you. When our Bratvas combine, we'll be the strongest Russian family in the Eastern Bloc outside Russia. Can you think of anyone who would have a motive to hurt you or prevent our wedding?"

"No, who all knew of the wedding? Only our family and possibly staff, maybe guards? What of your brothers?"

"We have always done what is best for the Bratva. Nothing can come between us. Don't ever cast doubt on my family or my family name." His tone is scary and intimidates the hell out of me when he's in such a snit at the moment. I'll never question his family's loyalty again.

I'm reminded Nikolay is a control freak and a powerful man who has a reputation to protect and uphold, and I have no doubt he will do that. I can forget about ever wiggling out of the mess I've caused by outsmarting the guards. It's evident we have enemies lurking in the shadows, waiting for an opportunity to strike, and they did. I shrug, feeling coldness creep over me when I imagine what might have happened had Nikolay not known where I was and rescued me.

Truth is, I'm to blame for this and should be thanking him. If he didn't own that club and have his spies everywhere, I wouldn't be sitting here gazing at his amazing bone structure and checking out his ass every time he turns his back. I admire his confidence and resolve. If anyone can find who's behind this, my money is on him.

"You're the one who broke the rules, and now you'll know what it's like to be a prisoner in my home." His delivery is as cold as his eyes when they meet mine. I hate being on the outs with him. I thought we were making progress. Now I'm not so sure.

"What about today? Kat and I were to shop."

"You will. However, Pavel, Alex, and I will be along to make sure you're not followed or taken."

My spine buckles at the thought of being taken, and I pull the blanket up under my chin. I've read about Russia and their torture techniques. I know I don't have the willpower to withstand it like Nikolay.

He hovers beside the bed, towering over me, using it to his advantage. "You need to remember your place, it's beside me, and it's non-negotiable. Don't embarrass me again with your childish pranks. I'm not amused. Now, go shower and dress appropriately for shopping. The wedding can't be delayed. We're in a race to beat the clock. Every day, from now until the wedding, puts us at risk."

I throw the covers back and leap from the bed, and thankfully his shirt covers my butt cheeks. My feet fly as if a swarm of hornets were chasing me. As soon as I'm in my bedroom, I close the door and catch my breath. Nikolay is as sexy as he is scary.

Overnight, my circumstances have changed. I am no longer as safe as I wanted to believe. I wanted life to be normal again, and now I realize I've been selfish, jeopardizing our future and possibly my life, over a few hours at a bar with a girl who turned out to not be my friend after all. I have to count on Nikolay to protect me, and as much as I hate giving in to him, I know my survival depends on following his orders.

Darci. I should have known something was suspicious when she was the first to befriend me at school last semester. Why would I ever be included with the popular students? I'm not a social butterfly like my sister. I was careless last night. I shudder to think of how badly things could have been. I'm grateful to Nikolay, yet I didn't thank him.

My head is still a bit hazy, and I have a pounding headache. I assume Kat is fine. I'll have to text her later.

Hazel appeared as if she knew I needed her.

"You're to take this aspirin and meet Nikolay downstairs. He's had to rearrange his entire day," she adds, as if I need another reminder of how I've ruined everything. God forbid the man is inconvenienced. But the look of disappointment in Hazel's eyes hurts me just as much. We're friends. She's the mom and best friend I always wanted, and I hope this won't ruin it.

Her words hurt me. It's the first time Hazel's eyes have shown displeasure with me, and the repercussions of my antics are delivered to me like ocean waves that keep rolling in with the tide. I wonder if Nikolay will allow me to return to class. If Darci knew my name, I assume others might as well. I bet she's mixed in with some scary men to do what she did.

"I'm sorry, Hazel."

"You'll learn," she murmurs as she leaves.

I take a quick shower, blow-dry my hair, and apply a tinted foundation to my fair skin, followed by a light bronzer. I wear a colorful blouse, skinny jeans, and boots with a zipper to make it easy to take them off and try on clothes.

I grab my small purse and frown. It brings back memories of last night's debacle. I make a note to get something different today. I finish the glass of water Hazel left and hold the railing as I go down to the foyer where Nikolay hangs up his phone. Pavel and Alex flank him on either side.

The threat to us is real. Having enjoyed life out of the public spotlight, I was naïve and out of my element to venture out alone. I can't risk losing Nikolay. If something were to happen to him, I shudder to think of what would happen to me, Mum, or Katerynia.

"Great, let's go," Nikolay announces, taking command of the situation. I follow beside him as we walk out the door without so much as a cup of coffee for breakfast.

I have no right to complain about being followed by personal guards. Obviously, Nikolay is the real target, but they will target me to get to him. If I'm dead, it will leave the Petrov organization vulnerable. I'm smart enough to piece that much together. So, someone in my father's organization is trying to overthrow Nikolay before he becomes more powerful when we marry.

I'm out of words as we're driven to the upscale side of London. I assume today will be spent without my sister's company.

"There will be no more talk about the wedding unless it's with family. Besides the few trusted guests we invited, it will be a surprise to the outside world. My brothers are flying in to help beforehand."

"Dmitry and Roman?"

"Yes, you'll like them, and if not, I suggest you learn how to get along without a fuss. A Bratva wife must obey."

"I understand," I murmur as Pavel opens the door, and Nikolay takes my hand to help me down from the high vehicle. His hand is warm and firm. To my dismay, he lets go of me as soon as I'm on the sidewalk safely. I look up to see the name of a famed designer on the storefront, a designer who only takes appointments, he says.

"Your wedding dress is here. You'll be fitted." His cold delivery bruises my weakening heart. I've never felt so alone.

"You can't see it. It's bad luck," I blurt out, immediately regretting telling him what he already knows.

"We'll wait in another room where we'll drink champagne. Afterward, we'll go to stores where you will buy everything from thong underwear to stilettos. The last stop will be a salon to have your hair done; you have an appointment this afternoon."

"What's wrong with my hair?"

He opens the door of the dressmaker's shop, and I enter. I'm overwhelmed by the sheer number of beautiful dresses in front of me.

"It's been a while since you had it trimmed, and it needs work. A Bratva bride has to look her best." He sighs as if I'm an inconvenience, and I suppose he has more important things to do than coddle me for the day.

If I thought he was controlling before, I'm learning what it's like to eat humble pie, and submission is the theme for the day.

"No wonder your father met an untimely death if this is how he conducted business." He drops that bomb before they are escorted to a different room, and I am left with my jaw dropping.

Did he have the nerve to diss my father as he lay in the ground? How rude! Granted, Papa wasn't my favorite person, but he was my father, and as such, I respected his place in my life.

A woman appears and introduces herself as Angela; she's British and is dressed in a pale pink business suit with pumps to match. I can only imagine walking around all day waiting on Bridezillas.

"Anya." I take her small hand in mine. "I have no idea what to wear."

"Oh, the big day is coming soon. We have to get to work. Don't worry, you look like a size six, and I have many dresses for you to choose from. I can make alterations so you'll look beautiful on your big day." She bubbles with more excitement than I can muster.

I run my hand over the silky fabric of the dress closest to me.

"Do you like this one?" she inquires.

"I like them all." I smile and try to snap out of the mood I carry with me. I find myself in a paradox because I'm marrying a man I resent for controlling me. On the other hand, he saved my life. Not wanting to think about it for one more minute, I decide to forget it so I can enjoy the day.

The dresses are astonishing, and there are so many styles to choose from. They come fitted or flared, sleeved or sleeveless, beaded with pearls and crystals, or trimmed in lace. You name it, and they have it.

"You would look beautiful in any of these, but I think you'll like something one of a kind. I have some couture made by a top designer. Follow me." She leads me to another room with only one dress on display.

"It's so pretty," I murmur.

"It's couture. No one else has it. Mr. Volkov requested it for you."

Of course, he did. Mr. Control Freak with his impeccable taste. How did he know I'd love this dress?

I follow Angela to a large fitting room where she helps me slip on the wedding gown, and it's no surprise the dress fits perfectly. I stare in the full-length mirror, and I don't recognize myself. It's true. I have let my hair go; it's unbecoming. I look at Angela, and her hair is perfectly coiffed into a chic bun. I need to look like her to be accepted into this new affluent world. I have a few clothes to get me started, but I need more to complete the look—hair, nails, shoes, and purse. All those things dictate how others will view and judge me and ultimately reflect upon my husband, who is... impeccable in every way.

Nikolay is not so subtly pointing out how inexperienced I am in life, and as much as I love fashion magazines and study them, it takes work and money to pull it all together. Stars have glam squads for their hair, makeup, and stylists for their wardrobe. It takes a village.

"Come, walk in it," Angela's voice brings me back to earth. I walk around the room; every wall has a mirror, and my reflection sparkles under the warm lighting. I feel like a princess floating on air. The bodice is a deep V cut, with a nude mesh showing skin without showing skin. I can't have every man in the room staring at my boobs. The waist is tapered. I run my hands down the sides to smooth the fabric, but it hangs perfectly without me needing to touch it.

Angela claps her hands together. "You look so beautiful," she squeals. "Mr. Volkov knew you'd love it." She makes me turn and walk so that she can see the view of my back as the gown sways with each step. I enjoy the material swishing around my legs, sleek and silky. I walk to the end of the room and turn, letting the gown's train follow in my wake. I hope Nikolay thinks I'm pretty in it. I can't wait to see my handsome husband in his tux.

"Do you like it?" Angela asks the obvious.

"Amazing," is all I can say as my body shakes with excitement and nerves. It's normal, I tell myself. I'm getting married in a week to a man who sees me as immature and incompetent.

It's a marriage I'm forced into. I remind myself I'm protecting my family. Nikolay is clearly the winner, gaining territories, money, and more power. It's a man's world. Even if I make partner in a law firm, I'll never be considered an equal. Nikolay hasn't mentioned it, but he will want children, preferably a son at some point.

I can wallow in self-pity or pick up the torch and run with it. I'll show him I belong by his side. I'll make him want me. In fact, I want him to beg for me.

"It's perfect. I'll take it." I smile as Angela fusses with the hem using pins from a pincushion she wears on her wrist.

"It fits you perfectly as if it were made for you," she mumbles. "I'm so happy you like it. Mr. Volkov said cost is no object, and this is the most expensive gown I've ever touched."

I'm learning what Nikolay likes, and the stuff I buy off the discount racks isn't going to cut it. A new day has dawned indeed.

CHAPTER 11

NIKOLAY

"*Y*ou can't see it!" Anya is adamant when Alex puts her black dress bag in the vehicle.

"Fine."

"You have good taste,* I'll say that much,*" she replies, getting in beside me.

"Hm, I do, do I?" I withhold a knowing smile. I know my little bird, and I can give her the world. I hope today she realizes she'll be taken care of as long as she's with me. I might withhold my love. However, I am a generous man with my money. She holds a special place in my heart, but she's not to know. I can't give her any power over me. No one can know my weakness is her face and companionship. The banter I complain about is refreshing.

"Pavel, take us to Bond Street, please."

"On it." The vehicle lurches forward when he steps on the pedal, and after a few roundabouts, we're at the premiere shops.

Anya is filled with glee and too proud to admit it. I'm amused as I watch her out of the corner of my eye. She's trying so hard to contain her excitement.

Once inside the store, I sit in the chairs left for men to use as I cajole her out of the changing area so she can model for me. She's having so much fun she is oblivious to how much she is turning me on. I can't keep my eyes off her. Pavel elbows my ribs.

"Shut the fuck up. I'm taking a day off." I try to ignore his ribbing.

"Sure, you are. You rarely take a day off. No doubt a blonde is to blame."

"Careful," I warn.

Anya is trying on lingerie and refuses to leave the dressing room. I walk to her stall, where I command her to open the door. She does so without rebuffing me. Is she warming to me?

"I'm not dressed," she says as she holds a blouse to cover her body clad in a lacy bra.

"I want to see."

"Uh...um," she stutters as her cheeks flush. She backs away until she is up against the wall.

"I'm to be your husband. I want to see what I'm getting in this arranged marriage, which benefits both of us," I add.

"That's chauvinistic, to say the least. I'm not something to be bartered. I'm in it to stay alive. After the incident at the club, it's obvious we are both in danger. If they get me, they can get to you." Her eyes flash a sharp blue before returning to normal. I've irked her.

I raise my eyebrows; it's an astute assumption she's making. I'll give her that. "I see you have the skills needed to think things through."

"It won't always be this way, me needing you for protection. One day, the tables will turn."

"That's quite the accusation for someone who blushes the second I find you in…" I flick the bra strap off her shoulder and pull the blouse from her clutches.

The look of surprise on her face is priceless when I unclasp her bra and cup her voluptuous C-cup breasts in my hands.

"Someone might come in…" she frets.

"No one will, and you know that." I flick my thumb over her nipple and enjoy how it stiffens with my touch. Her chest is visibly moving, her excitement rising. She's enjoying this as much as me. I roll my warm tongue around the areola before my greedy lips encircle her taut nipple. I suck it until she lets out a soft moan.

I continue to play with her nipple, clamping my teeth around it and giving it a tweak.

"Ouch!" She slaps the side of my head.

I chuckle. "You like that?"

"No," she exclaims, but her body says yes. She slumps against the wall, weak with desire.

I want to pin her against the wall and fuck her in this cubicle. The problem is we'll both be vocal when we climax, and everyone in the shop will hear it. Not that I mind, but on second thought, I decide to set a good example for my men standing fifteen feet away.

I reach between her legs to find her moist pussy full of her juices as I slip a finger into her, moving in and out as her body twists under me. She's no ice princess. I'll crack her like a twig. One taste of my hard cock in her and she'll be begging for more. No doubt her knees are having a difficult time holding her as her blood flows to her pulsating pussy. She will be experiencing a head rush from the endorphins. It's a rush I never grow tired of.

"Mm." Her moan is music to my ears.

"How much do you want me?" I search her eyes. Our lips are so close, and I go in as if to kiss her but hover instead. I can be such a prick.

She closes her eyelids, purses her lips, and turns her face away from me.

"You will want me." I slip another finger into her. She's ripe for a good fuck. She might be a virgin, but her body wants the decadent sex life I will give her. I have no doubt she'll writhe under me in no time.

"No." She struggles to get the word out as she desperately wiggles to get away from the pleasure my fingers give her as I hit her G-spot.

"You are trapped; give into it. You are mine. I own you. The sooner you accept the fact, the happier you'll be."

"I'll never be owned by anyone." Her eyelids fly open, and the moment is broken. I withdraw my fingers, licking them while she watches.

"Your pussy is sweet, pure. You won't be so pure when I've taken you." I move away from her. She covers her bare breasts and refuses to meet my gaze.

"What? No flippant retort? Has my krasotka lost her words?" I chide her in her moment of weakness.

"I'm done with shopping for the day."

"Fine. I'll drop you off at the hairdresser. I have some calls to make while you're there. Get dressed." I add that last bit to pour salt in her wounds, knowing she hates being told what to do.

I return to Pavel, and my cock is still engorged.

"I see you didn't fuck her silly." He grins mischievously.

"I want her first time to be special. I'm not an animal."

"Some might disagree," he muses.

"True, but she is to be my wife; some modicum of decorum is warranted."

"True."

Alex helps Anya as she carries arms laden with jeans, sexy bras, and matching panties to the register. I grab a few items of clothing the saleswoman picked out for her, but she didn't try them on. I like the cocktail dress and the skimpy bikini; she can wear them on our honeymoon. I also select more dresses she can wear to dinner and ask the woman to find shoes to go with them.

She scurries away. No doubt the commission on this will pay her rent this month. I pay for the items while my men load the SUV. I worry there might not be enough room for all our purchases.

The ride to the salon is without conversation. Anya is swept away by her stylist, Oliver, who was trained at the top salons around the world and has been summoned by famous stars while on tour in London. If one thought a normal day at the salon is expensive, one should see what he charges. Needless to say, he's lightened my wallet, but I'm told he's worth every penny.

I go outside to return some phone calls while Alex keeps an eye on Anya.

"Do you think one of George's men is behind the attack on Anya? Liev said he's been short and complaining about it."

"That's what put him on our radar. I doubt it, but it won't hurt to have him followed by one of our spies. Put someone on it. I want Konstantin monitored as well."

"On it." Pavel is a large man; traffic slows to let him walk across the street to a coffee shop. He grabs us hot caffeine as he talks on his burner phone.

It never hurts to be too careful. We have no clue who to watch. It's like waking up in a chess game before you realize you're moved into checkmate.

My phone rings.

"Roman, my God, how are you?"

"Well, brother, and you?"

"Living to see another day it appears. I can't wait to see you. Something tells me this is a quiet spell before all hell is about to let loose. I don't like it."

"I got you, brother. We'll be there soon. I'll do whatever you need."

"Great."

"I hear you're doing well." His tone invites me to add comments on my situation.

"Well enough. Anya was drugged at a club."

"How did that happen? I'm sure you'd kill someone over that."

"She snuck out, disguised as her younger sister, who looks more like a twin. The girl who drugged her is in the wind."

"Any read on who she might be affiliated with?"

"No clue. Can you go through the books I sent to you? They're encrypted. I want to know if anyone is skimming money."

"Consider it done. You know, if she's too much for you, I can make good on Dad's promise."

"That's gracious of you. I take it Mother has shown you pictures of Anya?"

"Of course. You're fulfilling the King's promise." Roman chuckles at the irony of me helping my father before he passed, and now I'm the king, still upholding the promise is ironic. I never dreamed becoming the King could happen so quickly. It's like a self-fulfilling prophecy, only earlier than I suspected. The getting married part was a long time coming. Nice of Dad to keep that secret in the vault. I wonder if he knew I had my eye on Anya years ago. All in all, I can't complain.

"I'm holding my own, thanks."

"Great, then I look forward to meeting your wife."

"And not me?" I pretend to be hurt.

"Of course you, too, brother. Blood and brotherhood can't be denied."

"That's the truth."

He rings off, and I grab a cup of coffee from Pavel. I wonder if my brothers will remember Anya. I'm surprised she hasn't mentioned her childhood, but she was young. Maybe she's forgotten me.

"Roman is going over the financials. Maybe he'll come up with a lead. Any sightings of Darci?"

"None, we ran her through Interpol. She's not there. There isn't a trace. We kicked in the door to her flat, in a terrible neighborhood. I assume she did the job for money."

"Still, it's an elaborate ruse to spend months getting to know Anya. That takes money. She didn't have it. There's no telling who is behind her or what they are capable of."

"I'm sure they're no worse than us. Hell, only the Chechens are worse than us." He chuckles.

I consider it for a moment. Some are within our ranks, but there are not enough of them to pull off a takeover.

"I'm thinking it's someone close to us. Who else would know Igor's guard, where he lives, and the fact that he must have called in that day so Igor would be vulnerable?" I run my left hand over my chin in thought before I sip the warm liquid.

The sky turns cloudy; the weather will be warming up soon. I'm thinking about Anya and fucking her on the bow of my yacht. My cock swells under my fitted jeans just daydreaming of it.

We walk inside the salon to see Anya sipping champagne as she chats with the hairdresser. One would never know this is not a part of her normal routine. She talks and moves her hands, growing more confident as she and the stylist connect.

I'm jealous and tell myself her stylist is gay. What the fuck am I jealous over?

The truth is I'm not into sharing. Even though I'm here, there are other men around, and her ring sits on my dresser. I bought a matching band for myself. Anya has a modest expense account. One I'll dump money into; as the wife of the heir apparent, she needs to be able to live a certain lifestyle, and it requires money to move in the social circles we need to be a part of.

It's late in the afternoon before we return to the house. Anya disappears upstairs with her loot. Pavel and I head to my large office and close the door.

My mind is preoccupied with thoughts of Anya in the dressing room. Her body under me makes my cock regret not taking her there. I'm horny, and I want what is mine.

I text Anya to wear a particular dress with heels for dinner tonight. I send another text, telling her not to wear panties. That should give her a clue to the evening I have planned.

CHAPTER 12

ANYA

Katerynia calls while I'm in the salon.

"Are you okay? I didn't tell Mum. I was worried she'd be upset." She's talking softly, so I assume Mum is within earshot.

"Everything is fine. Nikolay will handle it," I reply confidently.

"So, what happened?"

"It appears one of my school friends put something in my drink at the bar. It made me tired and gave me a wicked headache."

"How did Nikolay know?"

"He happens to own the club, and the staff tipped him off when I showed up without him. He got there in time to save me from who knows what."

"I hope he's not angry with me. You should've seen the look on his face. I would have peed on the rug if I were a puppy."

"Really? I was so out of it." A snicker bubbles in my throat at her graphic description, and it takes all my willpower not to burst out in a hearty laugh.

"Oh, yeah. That girl better leave the country if she knows what's good for her," Kat replies. "You should have seen the look on Nikolay's face!"

"Don't tell anyone, Kateryna. Swear to me you won't say a word. We don't know where our enemies are," I plead.

"Fine, I won't say a word." She promises, but I know she has loose lips.

I hope she can keep a secret. I have no other choice but to trust her.

"I have to go. I'm getting my hair done by a top person. I was afraid to ask if you could come. I'm not in a position to ask for favors after last night. Nikolay is reluctant to let me out of his sight."

"I wish I were with you when you picked out your dress."

"That's a secret too, the guests have been invited to a black-tie event, but they don't know it's a wedding, so say nothing," I repeat to remind her.

"No one is here but Sergei. I don't think he's capable of anything more than killing a fly. He spends more time looking at himself in the mirror than he does anything else."

"Hush! Don't speak of it again," I snap, getting upset at how flippant she's become so soon after Papa's death and after an attempt has been made on my life.

Did she forget how scared we were? Doesn't she know phones are bugged?

Hell, I thought someone was stalking me last week.

Being drugged wasn't fun. I never asked Nikolay if he had sat by the bed all night. He didn't need to. His wrinkled clothes confirmed he never left my side.

"I have to go," I say, "I love you," and hang up, returning to my day of pampering as my hair sits in foils for highlights. After two hours of a massaging wash, rinse, and toner, my hair is brilliant. The dead ends are gone, and I agree with Nikolay's assumption. The day at the salon was long overdue.

Damn, does he always have to be right? He has an eye for everything.

The shopping spree turned out to be more fun than expected. I never dreamed I'd make purchases in the luxury stores I've only dreamed about. I know the designers because I love observing movie stars, fashion magazines, and the people who walk the red carpet events on TV.

The wedding dress is something I never imagined I'd be wearing. I hoped I would marry a man who loved me, and now that's shot to hell. I'm exhausted by the time we return home. I'm in the middle of hanging up my new dresses when my phone dings.

Nikolay wants me to wear a fitted dress he picked out today and heels. No panties! What is he up to? It's not exactly how I was raised. Does he have a fetish for heels, for feet? No panties imply we're having more than just dinner. My heart lurches at the possibilities.

I do as I'm told and get dressed. I don't have to compromise my pride to fulfill his request. My hair is perfect, and I run my fingers through it as my silky tresses give way with little resistance. I marvel at what deep conditioning and trim can do.

Walking down the stairs, I hold the railing and hope to God I don't break my neck in these new heels. I'm surprised to find Nikolay waiting for me at the bottom of the steps as if he timed it. He's scary like that. I wonder if he has hidden doors in this mansion with the way he moves about, walking as quietly as a cat.

"Anya." He takes my hand as I stop in front of him. He's dressed in a dark blue suit, which goes with my light blue dress. I do not know what fabric it's made of, but I like how it hugs my body. "You look beautiful."

"Thank you. You look handsome. Thank you for today."

"My pleasure." He escorts me to the dining room table and pulls out my chair before hanging his jacket on the back of his.

Hazel brings us steaks cooked to perfection and thick-cut fries.

"This is so much food," I exclaim.

"You can afford to eat more."

"By the way, my sister wants to make sure you're not angry with her about the other night."

"I was angry with both of you, but we got to you in time. I don't know what I would have done had we not…" He pauses, waiting for me to say something. I meet his gaze, and for a second, I catch a softer, almost caring, look on his face before it disappears, and I wonder if I imagined it.

"Yes, it would have ruined the surprise wedding," I comment, deflecting what could have been an intimate moment had he not blown it. I'm not his number one priority. His family wants to save the organization and make it bigger and better. I'm merely the conduit through which he will accomplish it.

"It's more than that, you are mine. No one dares to touch you, look at you, or speak to you in any tone which I consider offensive."

I blink, startled by his sudden passion for my well-being. Does he care for me? Or is this another way for him to dictate my life?

I have nothing to say and eat another bite of steak. Nikolay is wearing a white dress shirt and cufflinks. It looks like his initials, set in solid gold. I don't think I can afford real gold for his wedding gift. He has spent so much on me. I felt a present for him would be nice on our wedding day.

Nikolay pours more wine for us. I take a few sips at a time, suddenly nervous under his scrutiny. The familiar smell of him, one which reminds me of my childhood, fills the space between us. It's as if he's familiar, only I don't know why.

The wine glides down my throat. I swallow hard; the room is too hot. I would rather rip off my clothes than admit that he is driving me crazy with lustful thoughts. My pussy is wet, and I hope I don't ruin the dress.

He reads me like a book, turning page after page, knowing what he'll find in each one. Instinctively, he places a hand on my leg and then trails his fingers up my thigh. I want to clamp them closed, anticipating where he's going with them from my experience in the dressing room.

I drop my fork; it clatters to the china plate laced with gold trim. I clutch the dining room tablecloth with both hands as if it will save me from his advances. I can't fall for him. He'll treat me like my father. I'll be giving up all of me if I let him in—in my pussy, my head, or my heart.

Doom looms as I know I can't resist him when his fingers play with me. Here, in the dining room, where Hazel could walk in at any second. It's a turn-on, and he's pushing my limits to break me.

I stifle a moan with my lips, but it's useless. The guttural sounds coming from my mouth are stifled moans of pleasure, and he's experienced enough to discern this. He continues to finger me, turning his body towards mine as his lips claim my painted lips. I secretly breathe him in, he's intoxicating. Possessive, demanding, and emotionally unavailable.

Damn if it doesn't make me desire him more. I long to erase the creases on his forehead after his meetings with Pavel. I assume he is plagued by tough decisions and stress to keep the organization bringing in money without exposing the Bratva. He's a criminal, and I'm falling for him. I hate my body for betraying me.

"Does this feel good?" he coos, his warm breath on my ear and neck sending shivers up my spine. His moist tongue trails up my neck and circles my inner ear. His teeth nip at my earlobe, under the pearl earrings Papa gave me on my sixteenth birthday.

I gasp for air as I wiggle in my chair trying to satiate the burning need between my thighs.

"Tell me you want me," he hisses against my waiting lips before delivering a trail of kisses all the way down to the top of my dress. He proceeds, pushing lower as he moves my lacy push-up bra, and dips inside to lick a nipple which causes me to shudder.

"No." I push the word out quickly, knowing it's a lie.

"You want me, admit it," he taunts me.

"No, I'm…" Fuck, I'm breathless. I close my eyes as if they will shut the desire burning between my legs. My pussy is wet, his fingers are a slice of heaven to a virgin who wishes to have her sexual desires satiated.

"You're wet, you want me. If you pull on the tablecloth another inch the entire contents of it will fall in your lap. Admit it!"

"No!" I shake my head, but my pussy clenches around his fingers as I inhale and close my eyes even tighter in my attempt to fend him off. My hands tug at the linen tablecloth bunched in my hands, and I'm losing my grip as his touches make my toes curl.

"Fine." He abruptly pulls his hand away, his chair rocks back, but rights itself and he storms out of the room.

It takes a minute to regain my breath. I grab my wine glass, gulping it like it's grape juice, and place the empty glass on the table, where it tips over because my hand is shaking. I stand, placing my hands on the table for support.

Tears well in my eyes. I hate to cry, viewing it as a sign of weakness. However, I can't hold them in, and they tumble down my face. I want him, but he can never know. Even if he takes my body, he can't breach my mind, or it's game over. I long for his touch, his approval, and instead, I get rejection because I won't give in to his demands.

I take a deep breath before I head to the staircase, using the back of my hand to wipe my wet face so I can see where I'm going. When I reach the landing to the second floor, Nikolay is there, bare-chested, his torso toned, tattoos covering his chest. A patch of hair between his nipples accentuates his broad chest. He's the Russian version of the Greek Adonis.

I tumble into his strong arms, instinctively wrapping my arms around him so as to not fall.

"What's wrong with giving your body to me? We're to be married, sex is to be enjoyed. I will show you." He kisses my forehead as a truce. My arms tighten. I'm scared but excited. He's given me an opening. One I can't refuse.

He kisses me again, urgently moving over my lips with a feverish pace. I kiss him back. My body is exploding with new sensations. I'm filled with curiosity and lust. My hands roam over his back, my freshly manicured nails digging into his flesh. I'm overstimulated and want him. I want all of him.

Our kisses grow rough, searching, exploring, and devouring each other. I gasp for air as our tongues lock, and he sucks mine into his mouth. He steps backward towards his room, and I follow. It's a dance without music. He unzips my dress—it falls off my shoulders and floats to the floor. I take another step and lean into him as I continue to walk, following him blindly.

CHAPTER 13

NIKOLAY

The intoxicating sweetness of Anya is the only thing on my mind as my hungry lips ravage her mouth and throat. Her lacy bra falls at the threshold of my door. I grasp her breasts, squeezing too hard, but I'm excited she's compliant. I'm sure she's wet for me. We're in the sanctuary of my room. I kick the door shut with my foot and slide out of my shoes.

"Sit."

She sits on the bed, naked.

"Unzip me."

She grasps my pants without complaint. My zipper glides down. God, how I love the sound of it; anticipation courses through my veins, and I moan as her hand grasps my engorged cock.

"Lick me." I place a hand on her head and brace myself for the excruciating euphoria of her warm lips on my cock.

She gently places me in her mouth and moves slowly at first, then finds her rhythm. I remind myself she's new to this, and I'm larger than most men. It's hard for any woman to take in all of me.

With one hand around my cock, she slips under my balls, and I groan as her fingers gently stroke them. Damn, it's my weak spot, and she's found it.

She sucks and moves her hand back and forth on my swollen shaft. When she flicks her tongue around the tip, my fingers grasp her hair, and I stifle another moan. Good girl, I want to say, but I remain quiet.

My body moves to her rhythm, and my back arches slightly.

I gently push her shoulders back, her lips slip off my cock, and her eyes meet mine, questioning my next move. With one arm, I lay her back on the bed and lean over her as she weaves her slender fingers through my chest hair. When I kiss her, she welcomes my tongue in her mouth, and we play a game of tug of war, but I'll always win.

I move on to her neck, sucking, nipping, and fighting my need for release. I want her first time to be meaningful. Her fingers find my nipple, and she slides her palm over it softly, then grasps it between her thumb and finger, rolling over it until it stiffens. She's intuitive as she finds her way around my muscular body.

Her breasts are perfect. I cup them and run my tongue around her nipples. I suckle on one, flicking my tongue over it again and again like it's a pickleball being volleyed on the court. It hardens, and a low groan of desire rattles in my throat.

"Mm," she moans, and her back arches. I rejoice in her submission. I slip my hand under her, pulling her body closer. Heat radiates between us, sweat breaks out on my neck, and my heart rate becomes alarming.

I slide my hand down her body, taking notes of her soft and supple skin as I make my way over her slender waist and curvy hips. I grab her buttocks, triggering a small yelp from her lusciously full and swollen lips, lips I adore, even when they sass me.

I slide my fingers between her thighs. She spreads her legs, giving me a wide berth. Using two fingers, I enter her. She's so wet I can't delay the desire to make her mine.

I pull back, and her hands move to my biceps, instinctively bracing herself for what comes next. I rub my cock over her swollen lips, spreading my pre-cum as she groans with pleasure. I enter her at last, slowly, hitting her barrier, and I feel for her for a second.

"This might hurt," I murmur in her ear as I thrust into her hard, breaking her maidenhood, and the thrill of it makes my cock more engorged than I thought possible. She's mine, and no one else will ever have her.

She gasps when I'm fully in her, but I'm in overdrive, lost in my lust for her. I thrust in and out, leaning on one arm to give my cock another angle as I shift my weight. Her pussy is tight. I'm delirious with my need to be filled. I can be a selfish bastard, but never when I want to please a woman sexually. I move into a sitting position, run my hands down her shapely legs, over her heels, and grab one petite foot. God, I love heels on a woman. I flick her shoes off to feel her soft feet under my large hand.

I lay her foot down and move horizontally before I thrust my cock into her again. She gasps as I fill her. I stroke her with my hard cock. I rejoice as her slick walls lubricate my shaft. She gushes, her juice bathes my cock, and when her body quivers, I know she's ready. I pump her harder and faster.

Her nails dig into my triceps, her breathing turns into guttural moans and groans, and she belts out a long 'ah' and climaxes, and her come bathes my cock that's buried inside her.

Her pussy clenches around me. Letting out a long groan, I explode, releasing my seed in her.

I collapse on top of her and prop myself up to not crush her. "You are mine, don't ever forget you belong to me."

I roll over, walk to the ensuite to clean up and bring her a warm washcloth. Fuck, I forgot about birth control.

"Are you on the pill?"

"Yes," she murmurs as she pulls a sheet over herself and uses the washcloth to clean up. Her face is flush with embarrassment as she stares at my still-engorged cock. I turn away to give her privacy.

A first time comes with sexual naivety and shyness with one's partner. It comes with the territory. Not that I'm an expert on deflowering virgins. I had one year after Anya left high school in my quest to become a man. I was left with a bad impression and a clingy female. Then and there, I promised myself I'd never do a virgin again, and yet, here I am, older and wiser, and I still fucked her. I got there first, and no other man will ever put their cock in Anya. Now to set some ground rules.

"I have rules. I never share my bed. I'll never fall in love, and we'll never spend the night together." My harsh words sting and her injured eyes are those of a bird trapped in a net. She recovers to return my glare, and her lips tremble as if she's heartbroken. I leave to take a shower.

When I return, Anya is gone, and all I have to remind me of her is the scent of lilies, the smell of sex in the air, and blood on my bed sheets.

CHAPTER 14

ANYA

My heels tapping on the marble floor is the only sound as I walk to my room in the quiet house. Closing the door, I lean against it as I shudder and gulp down sobs. I welcome the sanctuary of my privacy. Tears sting my eyes, eyes which used to be happy until I met the devil. He's so cold and remote; I despise him, and yet...I want him.

How could he make love to me and reject me so quickly? How do I guard my heart when I willingly give him my body? I hate myself but give myself a pass. I'm human. I can't deny how he made my body sing more gloriously than a Tabernacle choir.

Can I marry him when I suspect he may have killed Baran? What about Darci? What is her connection to me, and will we ever figure it out? She deserves to be punished for drugging me. Why does anyone want to hurt me? I have nothing to do with the Bratva outside of their blood running through my veins.

Nikolay and I teaming up to build the Bratva is good for both of us. Without it, my income is limited to what Papa has invested for us. I assume the money in the will is left to Mum. The solicitors will settle his estate around the time of the wedding. Judging from Nikolay's comments, Papa didn't spend his wealth on us. Does it exist?

Despite Nikolay's cruel words and demeaning comments, he prioritizes family. When we marry, my family becomes his, and he will protect and support us. We're stronger together. We both have something to gain in our union.

I run hot water for a shower, wishing to wash away the night. His sultry bedroom voice replays in my mind, and parts of my body still crave his touch. The memory of his dark eyes staring into mine in the dimly lit room gives me a glimmer of hope there is a human behind the eyes who can have a connection to someone. But will he ever let me in?

I can't forget what transpired between us. He's my first. I won't be another woman he tosses aside. His icy demeanor seemed to thaw in the heat of passion or lust. I'm not experienced enough to know the difference.

His large cock, imprinted in my memory, is glorious even by porno standards. Is it possible for a man to be hard after he comes?

Emotions and feelings complicate relationships, so maybe the wall between us might be good. Can I live with separate bedrooms? Without love?

Doubtful.

I hold back a fresh batch of tears imagining the lonely nights I'll have to endure. Will he be faithful to me? If so, for how long? Maybe I can barter and end our marriage. A year from now the Bratva will be under control, our threats will be neutralized, and we can go our separate ways. Surely, he will want that as much as I do.

I towel off, tug on my faded PJs, and brush my thick hair before I slide under my comforter with renewed optimism. I have to get away from him before he squeezes my heart into lumps of coal. Mum gave herself to Papa, and she's been unhappy for years. I'm guessing their arguments were about women, and I wonder how many Papa slept with over the years. They say once a man cheats, he'll always cheat. I don't want to end up like her—broken, alone, and lacking self-worth.

* * *

Nikolay is gone by the time I get up, which I planned perfectly. I decide today is the day I'm using the pool and make my way downstairs. Alex greets me and hands me a workout bottle with water.

"The pool is warm, and there is a sauna," he comments.

"Thank you." I take the container from him as he stands on guard next to the pool overlooking the backyard blooming with beautiful foliage and dwarf sunflowers in the shape of the letter V. We're enjoying spring temperatures in what will be an early summer. Luckily, we'll have a nice outdoor wedding without turning red from sun exposure. I let out a sigh. The wedding will go on as planned. I remind myself of the incredible dress I will wear and that I'm marrying the most handsome man I've ever met.

The large rectangular pool is surrounded by chaise lounge chairs comfy enough for an afternoon nap. The teal-colored cushions match the rolled towels stacked on a wooden rack. This house has every modern convenience and things I never dreamed of. I wonder if that includes an in-house movie theater.

I'm living in an elaborate gilded cage, but a cage is still a cage, be it made of gold or silver. For now, I'm sacrificing my freedom in exchange for my safety. When it comes to life or possible death, I choose life.

Wearing a skimpy white bikini I found in one of the shopping bags, I wade into the tepid water. No doubt Nikolay bought it for the honeymoon. The pool must be deep because I swim laps without my feet scraping the bottom. I detect a gentle current and notice tiny jets under my feet keep the water circulating without a sound.

I decide thirty minutes is a good start and get out, wrapping a towel around me so I can strip my bikini off without Alex seeing. He's a gentleman and turns his back, so I have a minute of privacy. I hang my suit on a drying rack and slip naked into the Jacuzzi, leaving the towel behind. I had no idea how amazing being naked in a Jacuzzi could be until today. The bubbling water makes the kinks in my body, left over from the events last night, disappear. I relax, take a deep breath and close my eyes, letting my body sink further into the hot water.

But it's Nikolay who haunts my mind even in daylight. I decide to enjoy the jets pulsating my tight shoulders and kneading my back muscles. After ten minutes, I wrap a towel around myself and enter the sauna. I toss a ladle of water on the hot stones and sit on the wooden bench, sipping the water Alex gave me. I'm refreshed and decide I can get used to this lifestyle.

The exercise, combined with the heat, makes me feel satiated and ready to tackle another day. God knows I need something to ease my worries and lusty thoughts. I'm sore down there and wonder if the way I walk and carry myself is any different. I'm finally a woman with carnal knowledge. I can't help but smile, knowing the women Nikolay has been with over the years have nothing on me. I've been with him, too.

Still wrapped in a fluffy, thick towel, I leave the sauna and proceed upstairs to shower. Alex follows close behind like a guard dog. He waits outside my room while I quickly shower, blow out my hair, and dress in a smart dark blue business suit Nikolay threw in my haul during our shopping spree. The heels I chose are higher than the ones I usually wear. I'm sure I'll regret them after an entire day. However, they scream sexy. I might disapprove of how our evening ended, but I long to have him inside me again. There was a connection between us, and for a minute, he was vulnerable.

"Alex, we're making a few stops today, and I have a long day of classes. My study group meets at the library," I inform him as I exit my bedroom and hand him the bag I carry to class. "We might go past dinner time."

"Boss won't like that," he murmurs, but he heads to ready the car ahead of me.

I stop by the kitchen to see Hazel and make a cup of coffee to go. She slides an omelet wrapped in paper into my hand.

"You skipped breakfast and need the energy," she says.

"Thank you, Hazel." I take a bite of the warm food. "It's good," I reply, complimenting her while covering my mouth full of food. I don't want to be impolite.

She shakes her head, but the approval in her eyes is evident. She likes me, and it brings a smile to my face.

Mom texts me the planning is all ready for this weekend's event. She has a headcount of forty people and mentions Sergei has been helpful.

Alex returns, then rushes ahead to open the car door for me. Even though men guard the perimeter and we live behind a high wrought iron fence, his head is on a swivel, looking for danger.

"Where to first?"

"A jewelry store. I want to get Nikolay cufflinks. Do you know what would be appropriate for a man with everything?"

"Family crest? Initials? A lion?"

"I've heard in the Bratva the crown is symbolic of the king."

"Possible, but today, anything goes. Why don't you use both your initials on them? That way, he can think of you when he wears them."

It would be disrespectful of me to tell Alex about my mentioned arrangement with Nikolay. I shouldn't care after what he did, fucking me and tossing me out of his bed like some sidepiece. Initials are for couples who plan to stay together forever.

I'm hoping our arrangement has a time limit. In the meantime, it would be smart to mark my territory where he's concerned. I wonder if there is anything I can do to make sure there are no other women in his life. I decide I'll use psychological warfare. I'll mark him in my own way.

At a jewelry store Alex recommended, I pick out a pair of pure gold cufflinks and ask the jeweler to inscribe the letters A & N.

Seeing as how Darci still hasn't been found, I no longer protest Alex going everywhere with me. I shudder at how easy it was for someone to trick me into letting my guard down enough to drug me. I never want to be helpless again. I'm learning to listen to my instincts. Darci dropped plenty of clues, and I dismissed them all. It's a mistake I'll never make again. Our fight-or-flight instincts are ingrained in our DNA for a reason. It's survival.

I blame myself for clinging to my notions of independence and realize my carelessness and inexperience in the Bratva world is a weakness that can prove fatal. I thought I was young and invincible. In hindsight, I could have been tortured or killed. My enemy is still out there and probably still wants me, dead or alive, I don't know.

I overheard Pavel and Nikolay speaking to Konstantin about the Irish making some waves and pilfering money from a 'boss' named George. I gather there is a separation of power within the Bratva hierarchy for protection should someone get arrested. The important men might know Nikolay's name, but few will repeat it. Those on the bottom won't know Nikolay's name, so it's next to impossible for Interpol to find him involved in criminal activity. It's an ingenious setup. It works, and that's all I need to know. The Bratva is different from most organizations regarding secrecy, making it difficult to infiltrate the ranks, and convictions are next to impossible. Nikolay should never end up in prison, and it is a comforting thought.

Cell phones are burners. There are dead drops like in spy movies, and together, the syndicate is savvy in operating lucrative crime rings.

The campus library is too quiet. I found my study group, and it's full of strange faces. I'm the odd 'man' out, and it's as if my life continually repeats in a social setting. Someone asks if Darci dropped out, and I have nothing to add to their speculations.

We review cases and work on a research paper about a controversial court ruling. Alex intervenes, telling me it's time to leave.

"No, I'm staying," I reply.

He gives me a worried look, opens his mouth as if to disagree, and closes it. He falls back, and I see him on his phone.

He returns. "Your fiancé demands your presence at dinner."

"Tell him if he respected me, he would respect the fact I have to work late, and I'll eat later." I shoo him away with my hand. He can deal with Nikolay. Better him than me.

In the back of my mind, I know I'll catch hell for this. But after his hurtful words last night, I don't give a fuck.

CHAPTER 15

NIKOLAY

*A*lex's text about Anya's refusal to leave her study group has my blood boiling. I thought after last night, she'd be wrapped around my finger.

I text her, Come home. Now.

My school and career are important to me. I'll be there when I'm finished, she texts back with lightning speed.

A heads up would have been nice, I yell in reply. I don't want her to know I enjoy our dinners. I've had years of eating with random women and eating alone. We were building a friendship. How could I have misjudged this?

"Pavel," I bark.

"Yes, boss?" He comes from another room, concern in his eyes.

"Sit, no sense in this going to waste," I grumble as I pour vodka, and we fill our plates.

"Good eating, thanks." Pavel is also single and married to the Bratva.

"What is happening with Konstantin?"

"All is going as planned. George is having issues, we knew of this. Liev is collecting funds, and your brother, Dmitry, is laundering them through businesses here and with crypto. He's got mad computer skills, that brother of yours."

"Yes, he has the mind for crime. I'm glad he's on our side," I agree without hesitation. We all found our skill set early in life. I'm wired for leadership; Dmitry, finances; and Roman, special ops and hits. Roman is a great utility man, filling in where we need him. Out of the three of us, he covers the most bases.

"I have been wondering about Igor's death. Who would have had inside information on his schedule?"

"I suppose that's why his bodyguard was murdered. No?"

"Maybe. I wonder if we're missing something. George alluded to the Irish wanting to shake us down over betting at the horse track. He wants a larger presence in gambling."

"That will be a cold day in Hell. We're in bed with the Chechens on that."

"Still, I think we need to talk to Konstantin; he's been here longer. Let's see what he thinks."

"Good idea, we'll talk to him tonight." I drop my fork and finish with the American food.

"I thought dinners were reserved for Anya." He digs for dirt. "Trouble in paradise?"

"I don't want to talk about it. Have you found Darci?"

"No luck there. We've reached a dead end. Fake identification and records are a dime a dozen these days. You know that. She's in the wind." Pavel slugs down a vodka and pours another.

"But whoever sent her our way is not."

I'm frustrated. We're usually on top of this in Russia. This job is turning out to be more than a full-time gig, and I'm busier than I thought.

"We need to make sure the wedding happens without any interruptions. I want our best team on security. What would someone want with Anya?"

"She's the crown jewel, no? Someone wants you to step down, it never changes. 'Greed is the root of all evil' is what I believe. Who stands to gain the most?" He shrugs and shovels bangers and mash into his mouth like he hasn't eaten all week.

"I think I need to go out tonight. Let's meet Konstantin and some of the men at the club, and get a read on them."

"Sure, might build morale," he agrees.

"Have Konstantin meet up with us in an hour."

"Got it."

I go upstairs to find something to wear that reflects my bachelor status. I'm a free man, and women are flowing like alcohol in London's finest clubs. Pavel drives me, but I wish I were driving my sleek Porsche. I waste too much time thinking about the most beautiful blue eyes I fell in love with years ago. I can't love, but how can these feelings still be here years later?

We pull up in front of the club, and a valet Pavel recognizes parks the SUV. Anya texts she's on her way home. I ignore her. She'll learn submission one way or another.

The sex club we run is in an upscale neighborhood populated by a circle of elites who spend most of their lives jet-setting to trendy party locations. Our club memberships are sold for a steep price, and it's a lucrative business. Russian girls looking to escape Russia know we have a reputation for not selling them, and we're never at a loss for fresh faces for the men.

As we make our way up the steps, we can already hear the music and feel the bass vibrating from the speakers inside. We wind through the crowd, men who know me nod and move out of the way as a sign of respect. Dancers and staff know me as the businessman who owns the club. The women, dancers, and guests look lustfully in my direction, but I don't give them the time of day.

We arrive at my personal VIP section on the top floor. A bottle of Cristal is chilled and waiting in a bucket of ice. Konstantin has done a great job with the place. From this vantage point, we can see the dance floor where naked girls work the poles and twerk for the clientele.

"Maybe you should bring Anya here," Pavel suggests.

This is not the place for the future mother of my children; however, he gives me an idea. Perhaps Anya needs more attention, like a night out. She's been cooped up at home or at school since her father's death. She's the only reason I want to go home, so why not give her a taste of a skyline dinner for two?

"Taking a woman tonight?" Pavel interrupts my thoughts. There is nothing stopping me. He gets the attention of a hot waitress and orders a bottle of the best vodka and the most expensive cognac in the building.

"Don't know yet." I'm still weighing my options. I'm haunted by Anya and the taste of her is still on my lips. My eyes search the room for someone to take my mind off Anya. I'm less than impressed, even though I know we have the most beautiful women in London. They are gorgeous, all ages, and sizes. Some have dark hair, others red, and plenty of hot bodies to fill my bed and suck my cock. And yet oddly, my dick remains lifeless in my trousers.

Fuck.

Anya texts. She's home. I know she must be curious as to my whereabouts. I don't respond. However, I yearn to see her. I missed her this morning and I've been working my schedule around hers so we can bump into each other in the kitchen in the mornings.

Konstantin arrives. We greet each other and talk about the club before he informs me the family will is to be read next week. Anya hasn't mentioned it. She might not know. I assume everything goes to her mother with the exception of trust funds.

"George notices an increase of Irish at the racetrack, he's worried they might be scouting it." He's a handsome man, and he leans against a pillar, which has thick red velvet curtains used for privacy.

"For what?"

"A weakness, possibly. I'm not sure. They are giving us pushback in areas where we move fentanyl. We're expecting more coke to arrive. Igor insisted we invest with the Italians to bring it into the United States. We also have channels to distribute it into other European countries."

"We help with that as well. I noticed from the flow of money to South America we're invested heavily," I reply.

I motion for him to sit, deciding there's no reason not to be friendly. His face relaxes when he sinks into the plush sofa sectional. The furniture can be made into a bed for recreational activities—the kind which eludes me tonight.

"Yes, we'll get deliveries this week with a steady stream from our Russian and Italian friends in the States. I'll make sure it all gets past customs. It's amazing what can be packed inside cans of fruit and vegetables."

"Isn't it though?" I muse. I like the man; he can't be a traitor. It makes sense as Igor's right-hand man to want my position. But my family's money, connections, and Igor's reputation and investments make us a formidable opponent. And, combined with our power after Anya and I marry, I'd say we're untouchable. All we need to do is make it there with no more surprises.

"Picking up women tonight or just watching?"

"Probably just watching, seeing as how I'm about to be married, no sense in pissing Anya off before the wedding." I run a hand over my mouth and chin as I make an excuse for my lack of enthusiasm for the scantily clad women gyrating around.

The club is entertaining even to connoisseurs. The wild clothing of the patrons and the array of fetishes, alcohol, and drugs provide an excellent cover to discuss business.

I glance at Pavel, who is hitting on our bottle service waitress. After she leaves, he opens the vodka and pours our shots into chilled glasses.

We toast in Russian, clink our glasses, and toss back the liquor. As the vodka warms my belly, I lean back and extend my long legs.

A woman approaches with long blond hair, blue eyes, and high cheekbones.

"Hi, I'm Cherry. Would you like to spend the evening with me?"

"You're amazing. However, you're too young for my tastes," I reply, checking her out from head to toe. After all, I'm human, and the guys can't know Anya is under my skin and in every waking thought. It's as if I'm a goddamn teenager again. I walk around the house sporting wood at the sight of her, and the inviting smell she leaves in her wake is like no other. Not to mention my heart lurching when she texts, even if her message pisses me off.

"No problem, I heard you were a VIP, and I wanted to introduce myself." She extends her hand.

I take her milky white hand in mine, and it's like Wonder Bread, soft, malleable, and nothing like Anya's, which are as strong as the retorts flying out of her mouth.

I stand. "Nice to meet you, Cherry. I'm sure you'll have a great night with these men."

"Where are you going, boss?" Pavel's eyes question me more than his words.

"Home, I'll drive myself. Put tonight on my tab and enjoy yourselves."

"More men are coming," he explains.

"Then I suggest you show them a good time," I smirk and head to the exit. The entire ride home, I'm wondering how to punish Anya. I don't know what to do. Do I push her or pull her closer? I can't fall in love, I can't break my rules on sleeping arrangements, and yet, I want her in my bed, preferably before I pop the zipper on my trousers with my hard... I'm horny as hell knowing she's home, and I'll likely see her.

The house is dark when I make my way up the stairs. I hear the TV in Anya's room. I knock.

"Come in," her sweet voice is singing a song.

I open the door to find Anya wearing a skimpy top with matching bottoms and get a full view of her firm, round ass cheeks. I long to bite on them, nothing is stopping me until she turns and disapproval flashes in her eyes.

"Oh, I didn't know you were home."

"Business," I reply as my jaw tightens. I'm like a puppy who doesn't know which direction to run to chase the ball without overshooting the distance.

"Sorry about dinner." She folds the book in her hand and puts it on her desk.

"Speaking of dinner, we're having dinner out tomorrow. Dress fancy, in a cocktail dress. Make sure you bring your passport. We leave at four."

"What if I have plans?" She bristles.

"Cancel them. Our wedding is this week, and we haven't been seen in public."

"I hardly think it matters." She stares down her nose, taking my face in. Her long lashes accent her large round eyes, and her pupils are the size of saucers. She's oblivious to how sexy she looks with her hair in a messy bun, and her long legs taunt me. I long to lick every inch of her delectable body, starting with her plump lips, tinted red from her favorite lipstick. Her nipples turn hard under my gaze, and my cock jumps to life.

Double fuck. I cross the room in three long strides. I pull her into my arms, devour her lips and neck, and rip her top off to reach her nipples.

I use a hand to clear her bed of personal items like a countertop full of clutter; it all lands on the floor. I push her cute bottoms down before thrusting two fingers into her warm, moist pussy.

She moans, her lips kiss me back, and her hands unbutton my shirt and claw at my flesh. I tug at my belt, then my pants, letting them drop to the floor.

"How dare you stand me up at dinner? You will always be home for dinner," I whisper in her ear.

"I had plans," she gasps as her back arches. I shove her onto the bed further, wrap my fingers in her hair, grab a fistful of it, and yank her head back, giving me complete control. I pull my fingers out of her and lick them as she watches with excitement building.

"You're so sweet, but you're mouthy."

"Likewise," she pants.

"Dinner or else," I reply.

"What?" She dares to goad me into a threat.

"School will be over," I threaten, knowing she'll concede.

I tilt her chin and wrap my hand around her neck, effectively making it so she can't move and has to look in my eyes. "We have to make this work. I suggest you get used to it."

"You get used to it. I'm not giving up my independence," she replies as her body melts from our body heat.

"Fine, I'm going to fuck you so hard you won't be able to sit down for a week." And with that, I thrust my cock deep into her wet folds and pump her hard, needing to release the cum in my swollen balls. She's ruined all other women for me, but no one will ever know. I'm the king. I can't have a weakness. She'll be my undoing of this I'm certain. Maybe not today, but one day, she will own my heart like I own her wanton body.

Her hands move to my neck, and she applies pressure. The look in her eye is that of a fawn who is inquisitive and curious, experiencing the world for the first time.

All the while, my excitement is building, and I'm torn between exploding in her pussy or giving her pleasure she can't deny. I put a thumb on her clit. Why choose?

Her breathing picks up, and her body writhes under me. I pump harder, going deeper and deeper, harder and faster. Her clit becomes hard. She is on the cusp of erupting. She begins to moan as a surge of pleasure simultaneously unleashes for both of us. She cries out and grabs my shoulders to withstand the power of my thrusts.

I let out a long groan and fill her with my seed. After a long minute, I tilt my head back and inhale much-needed air to restore oxygen to my deflated lungs. I have a headrush.

Fuck, fuck, fuck. This sex is insane. She's like crack, addictive, and I crave her and only her. I'm a junkie needing his next fix, her touch, her smile, not to mention the most incredible orgasms I've ever had.

I'm impressed her body can handle my insatiable sex drive, and she can fuck harder and longer than anyone I know. I pull my cock out of her. It's covered with her juices. I straighten myself, pull my pants up, grab my shirt, and leave her lying on the bed with a bewildered look on her face. Good. That will teach her to fuck with my head again. I'm over her childish antics and make my point.

This is why I prefer older women. They're mature, and I don't have to worry about unwanted pregnancies. I'm not ready for kids, nor is Anya. It's one area we both agree on.

CHAPTER 16

ANYA

I'm an emotional wreck when he leaves. Every time we have sex, I think things will change. He knew I'd give in if he threatened to take away school, the bastard. I cannot deny I love how hard he fucked me. Each thrust was deeper than the last, stroking the G-spot deep within, and I couldn't keep myself from moaning with pleasure. Once his thumb touched my clit, I was shattered, enjoying the rolling tides of euphoria I'd never experienced, even with a vibrator.

Fuck, our bodies burn hotter than the engines in a Formula One race car. I'm upset he left the bed again. In his defense, he warned me this is how it will be between us. I need to collect myself in the aftermath of the hot sex and head to the privacy of my shower.

A dinner date, he said. Did he also say to bring a passport? What does he have planned? I better look my best considering we might bump into one of his former lovers. My credit cards arrived this week. I do need more clothes. The sky is the limit. I'll show him how well I can fit into his world of affluent friends. With his insatiable sexual needs, it looks like a fuck a day is to be expected.

The hot water is soothing. I rub the soapy gel over my body and reminisce about Nikolay's strong hands grabbing me and pulling my hair to the point of hurting. I was immobilized, but I remember his controlling hold on my throat. His dark eyes flashed with excitement, or was it lust?

The entire incident turned me on. I wonder what other tricks he has up his sleeve. The man is mastering my body one fuck at a time. I'll show him I'm not the naive virgin he thinks I am. I'm going to flaunt myself in front of him, making him beg for my attention.

I turn the water off, grab a fresh, thick towel from the warming rack, and dry my body. With each stroke of my hand, I breathe in the sweet smell of Brazilian Bum Bum Cream.

I can't deny I love his body. When he looks at me, I'm over-whelmed. I can't let him discover his lack of affection is killing me. I long to be loved, needed...respected. Damn me for letting him know I'm willing to do anything to stay in school. I can't let him find out my body wilts under his gaze, and my panties are soaked with my desire for him.

Hazel has told me little about the Volkov family, but she did let it slip Nikolay prefers older women. I wonder if he will just use me as a baby maker. Will he be with others while I'm pregnant? I don't know his plans with me other than the wedding he drones on about.

I throw tonight's outfit in the garbage and pull fresh clothes, smelling of lavender, out of my bureau. I take stock of my closet and decide I will beat him at his own game. I'm going shopping for the most spectacular outfits on the planet, and when I walk into a room, all eyes will be on me. I text my sister to join me for a shopping spree tomorrow and fall asleep with the comforting smell of Nikolay in my hair.

* * *

"Gee, sis, this is an amazing car," Katerynia quips as she slides in the back with me.

"Thanks, but you know it's not mine." I give Alex directions to the stores we want to visit, and we're off on our adventure.

"So, what gives?" she asks with inquisitive eyes.

I shrug. "Nikolay has this weird rule to never sleep in my bed. It's annoying. Like, what is his problem?"

"That's messed up, but you know most Bratva men pledge a solitary life to their brotherhood. It might be like that for him," she adds.

"What do you mean?"

"He needs to stay tough, run the men, never have a doubt. He has to marry you, no offense." She shoots me an apologetic look.

"None taken. I never thought of that."

"Mom is happier now without Papa."

"Really? I'm not surprised. They've had a wall between them for years. I don't want that," I groan.

"I think there is an opportunity for you. You're not in love with him like Mom was with Papa. I never understood it because he repeatedly cheated on her and slapped her if she questioned it. I'd cut a man's balls off," she adds, balling up her fists.

Damn, if she isn't as feisty as me.

"What are we looking for?"

"Anything that will drive him insane in bed, an outfit to slay our dinner date tonight, and whatever else we can find."

"Sounds like my kind of day. Dad had me on a budget. It sucked."

"Oh, we're buying for you, too. What's a shopping date when only one of us gets to spend money?"

"Is he okay with that?" Her blue eyes grow wide with concerns of repercussion.

"I guess we'll find out. Judging from what he spends on staff and upkeep at the estate, he'll never miss it."

"Hmm, speaking of that, I can't wait to use your pool."

"It's divine. Any time." I reach over and grab her hand. I'm not sure if it's for her benefit or mine. Maybe I need the closeness of someone I love, even if it's my sister. She squeezes my hand in return, and we both smile.

We hit shop after shop, spending money like there is no tomorrow, and have lunch at the sushi bar in Harrods. We schlep bags of intimate wear, shirts, jeans, and shoes to the SUV. When we add our dress bags, the car bursts at the seams.

Alex drives us to the jeweler to pick up the engraved cufflinks. I hope Nikolay likes them.

While we're dropping Kateryna off, Sergei pops out to the car, taking me by surprise.

"So, how is life in the big house?" I can't tell if it's genuine interest or hard feelings because he wasn't picked to be my guard.

"Sergei." I hug him. "How are you? Gee, so much has happened."

"True; I miss your dad." His face grows somber, and for a second, I wonder if he's depressed.

"Me, too. But he would want us to move ahead with life," I add, trying to cheer him up. He takes Katerynia's bags, commenting on the vehicle. It sounds as if he's jealous, which is ridiculous. Papa paid him more than any of the other guards. I don't understand his attitude.

Sergei takes my sister's stuff into the house, and I take the opportunity to hug her and ask if Sergei is okay.

"He's Sergei, he's taken Papa's death hard, and he has dark moments from time to time. Stop worrying. We got my dress for the wedding and everything you need to blow every woman out of the room tonight. Now, go to the salon and get your hair done. You have to be home by four, or you'll screw up date night."

"I wouldn't call it date night, but you're right. I gotta run." I hug and kiss her. It's our thing, not a British or Russian custom. Alex drives me to the salon and hovers around, taking calls more than usual. I assume he's in touch with Nikolay.

By noon, I'm home, exhausted, and drop by to say 'hi' to Hazel.

"You have big plans tonight, I hear." She pours me a cup of hot tea. "Your hair is amazing," she exclaims.

"Thank you for the name of the hairdresser. He is amazing. However," I pause to give her a questioning eye, "I have no idea where we are going."

Her face softens, a smile floats on her lips, and my curiosity intensifies.

"You need to be ready on time. It's fancy, late dinner in a very romantic location. You need to look your very best." She gives me a sheepish grin.

"Do you know where we're going?" I ask excitedly.

"Yes, but I can't tell. It's a surprise." She averts her eyes to her hands. She holds the hot cup as if it's warming mitts.

"Oh, come on, we're friends," I implore her. I pull out a stool and sit beside her at the kitchen island where she eats breakfast. Her hair is always pulled back in a neat bun, all her dresses are floral prints, and she wears a white apron with pockets.

She rolls her eyes as if to tease me with the fact she knows and I don't. A chuckle enters the air between us. It's nice to see the glint in her eyes, and she looks happy for a Brit.

"Really?" I'm appalled she won't honor the girl code and spill. In her defense, it's her job, and she's mature enough to know telling me secrets could cost her her job or an unpleasant confrontation with Nikolay. I'm sure she's not one to pass on gossip, and so I remain without the details I want to know.

"I have my orders. Nikolay pays me." She gives me a stern look. "Now, dress pretty and wear high heels. Take your finest trench coat, and there is a gift on your dresser."

"A gift?"

"Yes, now go, get out of here." She steals my tea, of which I've only had six sips.

"Now?"

"You need to look like it's your wedding day. It's that amazing. I wish I had a romantic man like Nikolay." For a minute, I wonder about her personal life. I don't want to pry, but I'd like to know more about her. My inquisitive nature is never asleep.

"What about you? Have you ever had a great love?"

"The greatest, he was in the military. I love a man in uniform." Her eyes stare off as she recalls the past.

"What happened?"

"Oh, we fell in love, we traveled all over Europe, got married, had two kids, and he works in one of Nikolay's warehouses. He was so handsome. He's still a handsome man today." She shrugs with a sigh. "We're older. What can I say?" Her smile wanes, and the nostalgic glimpse she had a minute ago has faded.

"Surely you can have romance," I reply. I mean, is that it? One turns sixty, and life is over?

"Still in love, just not young enough to go dashing about like we did when we were your age." She pats my hand before emptying our cups in the sink. "Now, get going, and have a great time. I want to hear all about it tomorrow."

I leap off my bar stool to hug her. "Thanks, Hazel."

"Get out of here," she replies without hugging me. She doesn't have to; I know she cares about me. Who else would look up the recipes with me online and try them out to get them perfect? She's not one to use her cell phone for anything more than a phone call.

I heed her advice and mentally prepare for a night of what? I have no clue, but I hope it will be special. It's been a long year, and it's only May.

My fiancé, a romantic? Give me a break. He's anything but. However, it doesn't prevent me from taking the steps two at a time to get to the mentioned gift. What could it be? My heart races as I throw my bedroom door open with gusto.

On the dresser is a small box. I know that color of blue from tabloid rags featuring ads for expensive things I can never afford. I run to the coveted gift, lift the lid, and to my surprise and joy, I discover oval diamond earrings suspended three inches from the post, which is a lovely diamond in and of itself.

I let out a whistle. These cost a fortune, and I regret, for a second, spending so much of Nikolay's money today. I hold the jewels to my ears and look at myself in the mirror. They catch the sun's rays streaming into my room, and I'm fascinated with the magnificent colors of a rainbow dancing in front of me.

I gently tuck them back into the box. Nikolay must be thinking of me; why else would he go to the trouble? He's a busy man. I see him for coffee or tea in the morning and dinner, but with sex, he callously leaves me alone. He's never going to spend the night with me, and I don't dare to let myself think he'll ever compromise.

* * *

It's three-fifty in the afternoon when I walk down the stairs. I remember Grace Kelly, whom my grandmother loved from the old movies, and I hope I'm elegant enough to meet Nikolay's expectations.

The earrings move with me and tug at my earlobes. My black, elegant cocktail dress and heels are from a designer to the stars. I carry the trench coat over my arm. My passport is secure in my fancy purse. Hazel's never given me bad advice. I wish my mother could be my friend and help me. However, she lives more in the old world we left than the one we've built.

"Marvelous, Anya," Hazel beams her approval.

I thank her as I reach the marble floor.

"I have the night off, so have a great time." She turns to leave out the back as Nikolay appears with Pavel. Nikolay's presence commands my attention. His square jawline and cleft chin remind me he's as solid as his facial features. He's still taller than me when I'm wearing four-inch heels.

"You look lovely, Anya," Pavel murmurs. His eyes no longer scrutinize me. I assume he's accepted me into the fold.

"Thank you, Pavel." I had my eyelashes extended at the salon and look up through them to view my fiancé. Warm sensations wash over me like a low tide, and my blood warms in my veins.

"I'll be back in a minute." Nikolay brushes past me and zips up the steps. He returns a minute later. I can tell he shaved and changed; his cologne is fresh, and his eyes are bright, reflecting his mischievous grin. "Follow me." He puts his arm out, and I slip mine through it as he escorts me to the waiting car.

"How was your day?" he asks when we're on the road.

"Great, Katerina and I had fun shopping. I put a dent in the credit cards." The ends of my mouth curl as I remember the cost of my purchases.

"It's fine. You could buy a house with them." He glances out the window as the sun sinks in the sky.

"Where are we going?"

"You'll see." He turns to me. "How is the wedding planning going?"

"Kateryna says we're ready. Do you want a particular song from the DJ for the first dance?"

"It might be nice. What do you think?"

"Might as well put on the show." I shrug and breathe him in. Fire stirs between my thighs. I'm drawn to him. His sultry dark eyes take me in.

"You look beautiful," he murmurs as I melt like a chocolate bar under a tropical sun. "Hazel tells me you like history and art."

"Yes, I do. The British Museum is amazing. Everyone should know history."

"Ever been out of the country other than Russia?"

"No, I wish." My reply is demure. Did he compliment me?

"You're in for a treat." He smiles as our eyes meet. The moment we connect, the car stops at a runway.

What the hell?

Pavel parks and opens my door. Nikolay puts his arm around me, and we walk onto a jet.

"Make yourself comfortable," he extends his arm to the cabin of the aircraft, and I'm stunned at the leather recliner seats and what appears to be a room at the back. Holy fuck.

Pavel sits with the pilot, and Nikolay joins me on the couch as we take off.

"Are you hungry?"

"A little," I admit.

He walks to the small compartment and pulls out caviar and champagne. He pops the top and pours two flutes.

He serves me. "To my future wife, may we have many adventures."

I tap his glass with mine. What adventures?

"How is school?" he asks politely as he sits beside me and loads caviar on a fancy cracker.

"Thank you." I take it from him and place a cocktail napkin in my lap before I nibble. I'm afraid to spill a drop. I chase the food with champagne. It's a perfect combination.

Does he care about school, or is this small talk?

"You are on break for two weeks?"

"For the summer."

"Great, I have plans for a honeymoon getaway," he replies as he throws back a spoon of caviar and downs half his flute.

I sip the bubbly and remember one can get hit by the alcohol quicker at high altitudes.

"How are you doing in London? Any new leads?"

"None. Darci will never be found; if she is, she'll likely be dead. Someone wanted you, probably to get to me, but we've got more men watching us. I'm sure in time we'll figure out who the traitor is. It has to be someone close to the family."

"Good luck there. I've never questioned anyone close to us. Papa was adamant we had the best men on our security team."

Nikolay reaches for the bottle and refills our flutes.

His face is pensive with my words, then he brushes it off and focuses on me.

"Once we're married, we'll be the new power couple in London. You can attend school as long as you play my happy bride."

"A bribe? Have I not been a good sport over the ordeal?" I bat my eyelashes at him in jest. I notice the tent in his pants. It appears our sexual tension isn't in my head, and I smile, comforted by the thought he must enjoy our sexual encounters even though he likes older women.

"You've been well-behaved, I'll give you that," he concedes. His broody eyes soften as he observes every contour on my face, and I'm suddenly nervous under the intensity of his attention.

"Do I make you uncomfortable?"

"No, it's just..."

"Just what?"

"You have an intense gaze; I'm not used to it, that's all."

"You went to great lengths to indulge me tonight. Thank you."

"I need to be your well-kept wife, no?"

"That you do." He gulps more alcohol, and we're landing.

My eyes check the door behind us, and I wonder what's in it. I gaze out the window and watch the runway go by. When we reached our destination and exited the private airport, I noticed right away the signage was all in French. My stomach flips.

CHAPTER 17

NIKOLAY

"*P*aris?" Her breathlessness conveys the fact I made points with her. I won't fall in love, but her smile makes my day.

"Yes," I reply as we approach the waiting limo.

"Holy shit," she exclaims. Her eyes are on me, but I evade her look. It's easier to be aloof when I'm not meeting her gaze. I enjoy the excitement in her voice, and it makes me want to sink my cock in her again. I'm hard just standing next to her. Amazingly, her body fits into mine in and out of bed. But when we fuck, it's magical, like an elixir, and I can't wait to get my next fix. I never dabbled in drugs, but I imagine this is the high junkies get addicted to.

I don't know if I'll ever tire of seeing her face as she moans in pleasure under me. No one will even know what it's like to fuck her because she's mine. In moments like this, I relish the possibilities of what we can accomplish, and maybe the future will bless me with sons. Daughters who look like her would not be terrible. I can see little blond-haired toddlers with flushed cheeks and fair skin now. I've studied her enough to know every expression on her face. Every contour of her beautiful face is committed to my memory.

"The streets are amazing," she murmurs, taking in the cityscape as we move through traffic. None of this fazes me, as I've been here numerous times. I could have made this a business trip and checked on our clubs here. However, this week is busy, and this visit is to give Anya my full attention.

"The Eiffel Tower," I mention as we circle it. "We'll come back again to skate around it at night."

"You skate?"

"Well, I ice skate; here, it's on wheels," I reply with a shrug and mischievous grin. I'm a man of many talents. However, I do love outdoor and indoor sports. My cock twitches as I watch Anya's doe-like eyes widen excitedly as we pass Parisian sights.

"I'd love to come back and explore," she exclaims before we pull up in front of the museum.

"The Louvre?" She shoots me a quick look and turns away, but not before I notice her eyes are misty. I want to wrap my arms around her and share her excitement, but I'm afraid I'd lose a part of me I promised never to give away. No emotional attachment is my promise to myself. If any woman can change my mind on that, it would be Anya. She's the embodiment of elegance wrapped in finery. The earrings she wears dim compared to her eyes, lit with curiosity and childlike wonder. But she's not a child. She's a woman with goals and dreams who unknowingly saved herself for me.

And even though I was free to roam and party, I learned the business from my father.

The spell is broken when the car doors open. I slide my fingers in hers as we hold hands and enter the museum. It's a quick tour, but since we're getting married, this entire trip is designed to introduce her to my world of refinement. It's a glimpse into the world she reads about in her magazines, a world I can give her if she accepts it.

We take in the museum, pausing to read the descriptions under each piece of artwork. "You have a Mona Lisa smile when you taunt me and purposely do it. Why?"

"I had no idea. I don't taunt you. We have different opinions, that's all. I won't give up goals I've had my entire life. I'll be your wife, but I must be me, too."

I find her honesty refreshing. Too often, women will tell me what they think I want to hear. Anya doesn't appease me. I respect her honesty, even if it's not the answer I want to hear. The softness in her voice makes my chest expand. She's true to herself, like me. I don't deny what I am and my role in life; I'm married to the Bratva, my family. Now, she is joining us. I slip my arm around her and steer her to the most poignant exhibits. She's immersed in the art, and the happiness on her face is worth so much more than the cost of the trip.

"We need to leave now," I interject into the conversation. "I'm sure you're starving."

"I am," she concedes. She accepts my arm around her, and to my surprise, she slips her arm around me as we walk. It's a truce, but so much more. Why does affection from her put me on edge? It's a nice edge, one filled with excitement and possibilities. I never needed the thrill of a woman's touch before. However, I adore hers.

"Great, this way," I announce as Pavel makes sure the way is safe, and we head to a restaurant frequented by well-known celebrities. I've noticed the glamour magazines on the table in the kitchen. She loves movies because I hear them playing on her TV in her room late at night when neither of us can sleep.

We arrive at Guy Savoy's restaurant in time for our reservation. The tall, dark walls, reminiscent of another era, greet us as we're seated. The intimate dining room has glass-enclosed bookcases and large windows overlooking the grounds. A soft amber glow from the overhead globes cascades over Anya's light hair. I love her curious nature, and even though it's the most expensive place to eat in Paris, I'm happy I can indulge her.

"The movie stars eat here," she all but squeals, and her smile is more rewarding than overcoming major obstacles at work. This is a new experience for me. "How did you manage this?" Her eyes travel to the books on the enclosed shelves, filled with wonder.

"I know people." I can't hold back my smile as it blossoms on my face. I've impressed her. More importantly, I enjoy sharing my worldly knowledge, and she's appreciative. There are plenty of experiences I want to share with her in the bedroom, but that might take some time.

I order the best bottle of French wine, and we discuss the dinner menu, whereby she picks her entrée as I order appetizers.

"This is amazing. I didn't know you had so many connections." Her eyes soften as she peers into mine over her wine glass. We'll be married in a few days, and it doesn't seem like a sacrifice anymore.

"I'm resourceful. What can I say? I wouldn't be the Don without having a skill set to survive in the world in which we live. What's the point in having money if we can't enjoy the pleasures of what it buys?"

"Like me?"

"You're not bought, Anya. Don't diminish yourself. It's a marriage between families. We'll both benefit. Isn't that enough?"

She's quiet as food is placed before us, and I show her how to eat escargot.

"I don't know. I wanted to marry for love; you were a surprise. Papa didn't warn me."

"Hm, you thought he gave into your demands because you wanted it? No. It's never that simple. There is always an ulterior motive, remember that. Few give of themselves without wanting something in return. It's human nature."

"And what do you want?"

"I have what I want. Speaking of which, I've meant to give you this." I pull the ring out of my inner vest pocket. "I've been remiss in my manners; however, I picked it for you. Give me your hand."

She complies without hesitation, and the corners of my mouth curl into a smile. I slide the ring onto her finger. This is a first, and I take my time to hold her hand as long as possible.

"It fits perfectly," she replies demurely as she raises her hand and observes it under the light. I marvel at the enormous smile on her face, which is brighter than the gems on her finger.

"Do you like it? The sapphire reminds me of your pretty eyes."

"Oh, it's beautiful. Thank you, Nikolay."

I marvel at her genuine appreciation for a fine piece of jewelry. She doesn't act entitled like my side pieces, who are out to get as much as they can before my interest wears off. Anya is different. I never liked younger women, but she's more mature than most her age. She doesn't spend her life on social media or texting friends endlessly. I love that she's close to her sister and willing to make sacrifices for her well-being.

I cross the ring off my list of chores. It seems redundant to ask her to marry me. It's a done deal.

I turn our attention to the food experience, and the chef comes out to visit before we leave. Anya's face is flushed from the firsthand experience of what money can bring.

As we get up to leave, all eyes in the room are on us. We're the unknown power couple and the focus of everyone's attention. Shoulders back, chin high, she slips her arm through mine, and we make our elegant exit.

In the vehicle, Anya leans her head on my shoulder. It's been a long day. No doubt, the excitement wore her out. I kiss her forehead and breathe in her essence. I want to fuck her, my cock fills with excitement, but I let her rest.

I escort her to the jet, and after takeoff, I put her in the cabin in the back, laying her on the bed. I take her heels off and make her comfortable. I'm thrilled that I am the one to take her on her first trip to Paris. I thought she would be annoying like a kitten sniffing catnip, but instead, I found a woman searching for her identity and place in life. Her goals are admirable. Maybe she'll be able to work for us one day.

Anya walks beside me to the waiting vehicle, and we go home. At the top of the steps, she turns her pert face up to me. I'm filled with lusty thoughts. My cock is ready to rip a seam in my three-thousand-dollar suit.

"Thank you for the incredible trip," she murmurs dreamily.

"My pleasure. It's been tense, y'know, in the wake of all that's happened. It's nice to get out."

"Yes, it was," is all she can eke out before my lips crush hers. Her red lipstick won't be tidy after our lips devour each other, and my tongue enters her mouth. She doesn't fight me. I no longer have the battle of wills, and my tongue dominates her mouth before moving to her neck, where I suck overzealously. I curse to myself. I don't want to mar her silken, perfect neck with a hickey. On the other hand, I'm marking my woman. There is no doubt she's mine, now and forever.

I scoop her into my arms, and her arms slide around my neck as she nuzzles my chest. I wish I could feel her skin on my chest and curse my shirt with a million buttons and cufflinks. I can't get to my bed fast enough. Once I toss her on my bed, I unclasp the cufflinks and throw them on my bureau, then shuck my clothes with haste, kicking my shoes off without a care as to where they land.

"Say it," I command as I peel off her finery. I caress her feet before removing her heels and tossing them to the floor.

"Fuck me." She emphasizes the 'Fuck,' making it clear she's ordering me.

My cock springs from its confinement as my pants drop. I pull her naked body to the edge of the bed and kneel on the cool marble floor. I run my lips inside her drenched pussy, and lap her up like she's my favorite whiskey, only she's sweet. I moan and dive deeper, and her back arches off the soft duvet. Her hands grab my head and move it to where she wants it to go—a woman who knows what she likes and conveys it.

I oblige and place my thumb on her clit, stroking it as she murmurs inaudible words and groans.

"Don't come."

"Mm," is all she communicates. I stand over her now. My throbbing cock swells inside her warm pussy. She's waiting for me, and her back arches as if to bridge the distance between us. I smile in the darkened room. She wants me. But I hold back. Teasing her will make her orgasms more intense. And I mean to give her more than one.

"Now," she moans eagerly.

That's all I need to know to satisfy my desire. I thrust into her again and again. Her pussy is tight against my veiny cock. The glorious sensations as I sink balls-deep in her pussy turn me on even more. Her wetness soaks my cock. I lie in a prone position over her, my lips covering her nipple, and my hand grabs a large breast, giving it a squeeze as we find our rhythm. Her pussy constricts my cock, and I groan with pleasure, and we both explode, riding the crest of a twenty-foot wave called ecstasy.

She calls out my name, and I like hearing it roll off her lips—soft, sultry, and euphoric.

Damn, she's hot as fuck, and I don't know if I'll ever have enough of her. I'm exhausted from our lovemaking. I'm physically, mentally, and emotionally drained as I pull her to me. As I drift to sleep, I revel in the possibility that she is the perfect woman for me.

CHAPTER 18

ANYA

*I*t's dark when I wake. Was last night a fantasy? Did I really visit the Louvre? Paris, the city of love. I let out a soft sigh at the memory of our official first date. Is Nikolay growing a heart? I run my fingers over the gorgeous ring; the edges of the diamonds are squared off, it's surreal how large it is on my petite finger.

He is romantic! My head spins; this ring is worth more than my car. I take that back, more like ten of my little Jettas. Judging from his demeanor yesterday, he obviously doesn't care how much he spends on me. I couldn't care less about how he makes his money. However, I know where greed led my father, and I don't want Nikolay to meet the same fate.

Assuming I'm in my own bed, I'm confused when I open my eyes and see a room filled with dark wood furniture, presumably antiques. There is an armoire with a long mirror on one door. The moon was full last night, so it must be close to dawn judging by the shadows creeping in between the window blinds.

My heart skips a beat. Why am I still in Nikolay's room? Did he change his mind on sleeping arrangements? Or is this a one-time event? I gently roll over, expecting him to be gone, but he's sleeping peacefully beside me. I take a minute to observe him, unencumbered by his intense eyes. I take in his relaxed face as he sleeps soundly. My heart soars. He let me stay the night. Surely, this means something.

I watch his chest rise and fall. The scruff growing on his chin and cheeks is sexy. The faint but familiar aroma on the pillowcase hits my nose. I recognize the mystery scent now. It's from the sage flowers in Russia. That's what is familiar about him! My father is from his town, but we moved when I was young. The flowers cover the countryside and are used as fragrances in natural soaps and colognes.

We must have known each other as children. I force my mind to go to the past. Yes, vaguely, I remember a teenage boy who pulled on my braids! We were friends with the Volkovs. We all walked the same path home from school. He was handsome then, and I must admit I had a crush on him.

What might have happened to us if we were left to our own devices? Would we have fallen in love? Would we have had a future together had my family stayed?

Maybe, we were meant to be together all along. What are the odds of us being forced together after all these years? I mull this over, stunned by the revelation he liked me when we were young. I wonder if he remembers. As if I will it, his eyes flutter. I prop my elbow on the pillow and use my hand to support my head.

Dawn streams into the room. I've learned Nikolay spares no expense where I'm concerned. I know he enjoyed last night because

I saw his eyes dance every time I expressed my excitement about the exquisite art, the incredible food, and the luxurious private jet.

Papa never let us fly with him. He said private jets were for work, not pleasure. Now, I realize he could afford it and we could have had many luxuries, but he was a selfish man. Nikolay was right, Father gave me what I wanted because in the end, he knew I'd be responsible for the family. To do so, I'd have to marry to strengthen the family's security and, of course, the finances.

"Good morning." Nikolay stirs, reaching out an arm and softly pulling me to him. I succumb to his seductive voice and lay my head on his bare chest. His hair is tousled, and I can't help but smile at the satisfied and peaceful look on his handsome face. Granted, we made love several times last night and I had numerous orgasms. I had no idea it was even possible. I'm a bit sore, but I revel in it because he wanted me over and over again.

"Good morning," I reply, and for the life of me, I don't know why my face flushes. We've been experimenting with sexual positions, and for now, I'm happy he can't see my face. I'd hate to give my emotions away.

"What's on the agenda for today?" He plays with my hair, running his fingers through it as if lost in thought. Normally he's on a strict schedule and racing out the door without so much as a 'goodbye'. Morning conversations are limited to business, facts, and giving orders.

"I have to check on the wedding details and enroll in classes for the fall semester. You?"

"Mm, I think I want to spend another hour in bed and make sure you remember me all day."

I glance up and catch a sultry flicker in his eyes and instinctively know the sheet is making a tent over his hard cock.

"Do you, now?" I tease.

Oddly, this feels natural. Isn't this what married life is supposed to be? Communication, romance? Dare I allow myself to fall in love with him?

He gently strokes the side of my face with his fingers, fingers I love, and I'm wet between my legs. He peers into my eyes; lust radiates off him like the heat of a generator.

He leans into me, kissing me slowly, taking his time to lick my lips and map out my mouth. My tongue wraps around his tongue, and like a slow tango, we take turns sucking on each other. His low moan fills the room, and I grab his cock, wanting to take it in my mouth.

I crouch into a position so I'm kneeling in front of his cock and run my hand down his shaft to the base. I run my tongue around the tip, slick with his pre-cum. He moans again. I slide a few fingers under his balls, gently rubbing over the stubble growing back from his manscaping. The girls at school said men like this. He gasps and sucks air through his perfect teeth. I run my hand up and down his cock before I slip him inside my mouth.

He places his hand on my head, guiding me to a tempo he likes. His body stiffens, and his cock swells, filling my mouth as I clamp my lips around him to apply pressure even though he's slippery.

I bob my head again and again until he lets out a long guttural moan and shoots his wad. I swallow, but it's not enough, more is coming, like a river overflowing. I swallow again and warm cum slides down my throat, leaving a salty taste on my lips.

"You did very well," he commends me, and for once, it's a compliment without a cut-down.

"Mm." I lay my head on my pillow and wonder when he will get up. I'm shocked when he flips over and buries his head between my legs.

"I think it's only fair you get to come, too," he murmurs as he licks my wetness. My nipples grow hard under his expert touch. My juices seep past my engorged lips. His tongue flicks over my clit, and I can't refrain from lifting my ass off the bed as I yearn for more friction.

"You're greedy," he comments before he inserts two fingers in my vagina. I ride him as he strokes my inner goddess perfectly. We're like a well-rehearsed symphony; his tongue hits all my buttons, and euphoria wells in my pussy as it clenches around him.

"Come," he commands.

Desire builds in my belly, hot blood pumps through my veins, and my head is floating in the clouds, oblivious to anything other than the euphoria rising like a tsunami in my pussy. I ride the wave to the top and explode, gushing over him as I cry out his name. I pull at his hair, my body goes taut, my back arches, I strive for the last hard pass over my clit where his fingers massage my G-spot and I come again, squirting into his mouth as he laps me up like a thirsty dog.

My body was suspended in the air, but after the second wave of orgasms, I'm exhausted. I sink into the bed, spent.

"How was that?" I can't tell if he's mocking me, but as long as he makes me climax like that, I don't care. I'm addicted to him, his magnificent cock, and how he makes my body and soul bellow with pleasure, releasing my pent-up sexual needs.

"Amazing," I purr. I'm weak from my desire for him, and I wilt under his touch. I'm lucky my future husband wants to fuck me. I want to live in this cocoon we've encased ourselves in for the last twelve hours. I don't want it to end but know I'm being unrealistic.

"Good," he says and springs out of bed. "I have a full day ahead of me. I'll see you at dinner, you can go."

And like that, my world crumbles again. This is his cue for me to leave.

"You don't have to be so fucking rude," I exclaim as I leap from his bed. I collect my clothes and shoes which are strewn about the room. I leave in a huff, slamming the door behind me.

Why does he have to ruin everything? It's only a matter of time before I retaliate. I'm not going to put up with his bullshit. I will not be my mother; I will not be his doormat. I'm to be his wife and he damn well better respect me, or this deal is off, and I'll take my chances with the consequences.

CHAPTER 19

NIKOLAY

I'm such a bastard. Anya is sweet, and oddly, she's been more accommodating than I expected. I'm sure she's making the best of the situation by simply doing what I want. The trip to Paris was enjoyable, so much so that I let my guard down and broke my rule about sharing my bed all night. I wanted to stay in bed with her longer, but somehow found the willpower to break her spell over me.

My mother will fly in the night before the wedding and stay in London while we're away on our honeymoon. In the wake of Dad's passing, it will be good for her to visit friends and take her mind off things.

I'm stressed we haven't found the traitor in our midst. I've put more men on the security detail to make sure the wedding goes off without a hitch. This marriage is a coup and will strengthen and solidify the future of our families.

I've discovered Igor had drug deals in the works, and we can incorporate them into our supply chain as well. In Russia, we are far from ocean access, and it puts us at a disadvantage when it comes to keeping costs down when we have to rely on others to bring contraband through ports and across miles of road by trucks.

Anya throwing a fit and slamming my bedroom door amuses me. If she thinks she's pissed me off, she's wrong. I like the way she speaks her mind and expresses her feelings. Just as long as she does it when we're alone and not in front of Konstantin or the brigadiers.

Pavel knocks and enters. "Trouble in paradise?"

"Nothing another hard fuck won't cure," I reply as I walk around butt naked and peruse my large custom closet built for two.

"Your brothers are arriving today. You should be finished with your meetings before they get here."

I don't know what I'd do without Pavel keeping my schedule. I have other things to worry about. I need to make alliances and keep business partners happy to run the empire. He can worry about the logistics of getting me where I need to go and making sure our locations are safe. Granted, I have corporate offices, but some deals are done in an alley behind our club to ensure we're not being recorded. We have the added security of knowing where all the CCTV cameras are hidden. Technology constantly infringes on our world, and car trackers hear every detail and can be stowed in the most innocuous places. It means we are vigilant in daily sweeping all the vehicles, offices, and houses.

"Right, well, I'll be downstairs if you don't need anything." I can't miss the smirk on his face and a raised eyebrow when he does a double take on the messy bed. It's obvious Anya spent the night. The sheets are tossed on both sides, and the smell of sex still hangs in the air.

"Don't go there. I'm not going soft. I was tired, and Paris, well, it's my weakness."

"Tell yourself what you like; my money says Anya is getting under your skin and into your head."

"Get the fuck out," I quip.

"Going," he replies as he closes the door behind him.

I shower, hoping to rinse off her lavender scent. I can't walk around smelling her and not get an erection. Damn, Pavel is right. She's changing me one tiny detail at a time. A day off? Me? No one would believe it. A memory of her in Paris pops into my head. Her eyes were closed, and her head was tilted back while eating scrumptious delicacies at the restaurant. Clearly, she likes the finer things my money can buy. But is her heart warming to me?

Why does it matter?

It fucking matters. I noticed men checking her out as we walked through the dining room last night. Granted, the earrings were stunning, but they pale against her beauty. She has no idea of the effect she has on men, and she's not a bitch like most women in affluent circles. Most women in our wealthy circle have to have the best of everything, from the location and size of the house, the most expensive cars, loyal staff, and near-famous cooks.

They will talk sweetly to Anya's face but have a dagger poised to stab her in the back. These hyenas circulate in the same social circles as us, and Anya will never see them coming with their digs filled with jealousy and talking behind her back about her outfit not being up to snuff even though nothing is wrong with it. I will need to run interference for her and have the few women I've befriended over the years watch over her. The jet-set life resembles Noah's Ark because everyone has to be a couple, especially for women. It's a double standard, but true in this case.

I have nothing to do with these people because their social circle provides me access to elected officials and investment partners. My family constantly strives for legitimacy in the eyes of society and the law. Perception is reality, and I'm milking that teat for legitimacy.

As for Anya, I'll vet her friends; she'll never know about it as Pavel will do it behind the scenes. I, on the other hand, need to be in the know. I'll always worry about her safety. It's best to mitigate it by overseeing it myself, but I don't have time. Alex can do the everyday detail, but I'll have his balls in a guillotine should something go wrong on his watch. I can't risk anything happening to her. I'm falling in lust with her because love is out of the question, even if she's held a special place in my heart since we were kids. I thought I could live without seeing her again. At times, I wished I hadn't, but fate intervened, putting us together again.

I buy what I want and have a garage on the estate filled with the most expensive sports cars. The only thing I deny myself is love. I can't allow myself the luxury or heartache when it's no longer returned. I already broke a rule by letting her stay in my bed last night. It can't happen again.

I dry off from the shower and dress professionally before I meet Pavel downstairs. The day is filled with contractors we need to refurbish old offices we will rent and legitimate business associates for a new club we are opening later this summer.

I'll be short on time and decide a short honeymoon will have to suffice. I want to be at sea so I can bend Anya over the bow of my yacht and fuck her. I'm sure the tabloids will notice us, and the type of publicity will get my name in front of the men I want to meet.

I wasn't surprised when the pictures of her deceased father appeared online, and on the side was a snapshot of us walking out of her flat the day we met again. The 'mystery man' they call me.

Little do they know, they've spotted the new king of the Volkov Bratva.

I head to the kitchen, hoping Anya will be here to see me off. It's an unspoken ritual we have, and I've grown accustomed to it. My heart beats faster, and my blood pressure rises, as does my cock.

Pavel is slouched against the cupboards but straightens when he hears my shoes on the cold marble floors. He pours me a coffee.

"Pavel, any word on the reading of the Petrov will?" I take the mug of black coffee and bring it to my lips, wondering if Anya will appear before we leave.

"Yes, it will take place Monday, after the wedding. What's up?"

"No matter, I'm just curious. It's not like us to be in the dark this long. Has Dmitry cracked into the files? I don't want any surprises."

"He might have news when he arrives. I know he was working on it. He's traced facial recognition cameras from CCTV for Darci; all he's discovered is her going to and from school and the grocery store. After the incident, she was seen leaving her apartment, some seedy dump in the East End of London."

"Mm. Yes, we move lots of drugs there. In fact, I'll have to dispatch Dmitry to New York after the wedding to team up with our Bratva connections there. Dad was trying to broker a deal with the Italians to get more fentanyl into the city. From there, we'll move it west to Chicago and east to the coast. The Cubans control the Miami ports. I don't want to mess with cartels. I'd rather have someone else be the buffer."

He nods, respecting my thought process. "Are you working with the Morettis?"

"Yes, it appears Dmitry has friends in New York and ties to the Moretti's from boarding school, something about a beef in a bar during spring break at some snotty resort." I chuckle, leaving it to him or Roman to find trouble at any hour of the day or night. Dmitry cannot back down if he feels he's been played at a poker game or set up in a pool hall. I don't know why wise guys push the envelope. It's in their DNA. They can't pass up a hustle. Russians tend to remain low-key unless too much vodka is involved. Making detailed plans and executing them with laser-like precision is the key to staying under the radar. Get in, get out, and don't blow it.

The Italians in America are more flagrant. The more I mull it over, I need boots on the ground. There's no room for error. I'll send one of my brothers to handle the deal to make sure the Italians don't fuck it up. Three million dollars is our buy-in, and that's only our end of the deal. It would be a good haul to pick off if our enemies knew it was coming. One fucked-up shipment can put our neck in the noose. We have fences waiting on this delivery in numerous countries, and they aren't the type of men I want to piss off.

Hazel busies herself at the gas stove, and the comforting aroma of ham and eggs swirls in the air while I anxiously eye the doorway. Will Anya show up, or is her nose bent out of joint? If it is, how do I fix it? Why do I care? She's addicted to sex like me; we can't resist each other.

"You know, if you keep pissing her off, it will only build resent-ment. You need her as much as she needs you. Would it be so bad to be pleasant?" Pavel asks, and he has a point. I'm happy he's the only one to notice my disappointment when the piercing blue eyes don't join us for breakfast.

"Remember who you're talking to," I bark as Hazel slides plates of eggs, fried potatoes, toast, and ham under our noses. A pot of hot tea, coffee, cream, and sugar is already on the table in the breakfast nook.

"Aye," he replies, stuffing a piece of buttered toast in his mouth. Dressed in a black polo and slacks, his gun is clipped to his belt, and his cell phone lies on the table.

I'm in a gray suit for my business meetings. "Have someone pick up my tux from the cleaners. Our wedding bands are in the safe. I can't believe it's finally happening."

"You knew you were to be married off. You had a good run," he adds, scraping the yellow yolk off his plate with another piece of wheat toast.

"Fuck," I mutter. She's still not here. I'm in charge, fuck this! I'm tired of waiting. "Summon Anya, I might have to add mandatory breakfast to the schedule."

Pavel wants to grin as he knows she's getting under my skin, but he knows to keep his mouth shut and the smirk off his lips.

"On it," he replies as he pushes back his chair and heads out without delay to fetch my fiancée.

Minutes later, I hear voices in the hall. I'm immediately at ease when the sound of her voice echoes off the empty walls. This is more like it. I gulp the last of my coffee and slick my hair back with my hand. What the fuck am I doing? I'm nervous. I never get anxious over a woman.

"Anya." I stand. "Good morning."

"If you say so." She bristles and stands next to Hazel, flipping her sunny-side-up eggs out of the cast iron skillet and onto a white plate.

"I do." I sit. "I apologize for my abruptness this morning. I'm not used to sharing my room." There, enough said.

She shrugs and grabs a teacup before joining us at the table, but she sits next to Pavel, not me. She's still pissed.

"Just a reminder, you can redecorate the house if you like. Make it comfortable for you. We're living here, not my mother, as much as I love her," I add. There, that should make her happy. It crosses my mind she might max out that credit card just for spite. However, I'm not concerned. I deserve it, but I know she's not the type to do something so immature. As for her shopping sprees, she hasn't figured out that I benefit from her lingerie, and her new closet filled with clothes will be needed for the places I will take her to show her off.

The memory of her red push-up bra matching her lacy thong makes my cock jump. I'm surprised it doesn't provide a knocking sound under the table. I busy my hands with my food, which has grown cold, but I pretend it's fine to keep my mind clear and my hands occupied.

"We'll have our wedding announcement in the paper with pictures after the ceremony. Our short honeymoon in the French Riviera is set, and after that, I'll need you to join some charities. Philanthropy is good for business. I'll leave a list for you. Also, my brothers are arriving today. Dinner will be an opportunity for you to get to know them."

"Do they share your charming personality?"

"I'd say they are more forthcoming than Nikolay," Pavel interjects. I'm sure he intends to reassure Anya they aren't all grumpy like me, and he's trying to smooth things over. I've been demanding. I need her in a good mood for the busy week. It's important to me she makes a good impression on my family. It didn't matter before, but now that I've had her in my bed, it's suddenly important for my family to like her.

I remember Anya and her sister from our humble beginnings. She watched over her sister then like she does today. I had a crush on her, in fact, I'd masturbate to her lovely face, but she was too young to date. I wonder if she remembers. I keep this information to myself. I'm rebuilding my wall of indifference so I won't be compromised in the face of threats.

She's effectively weakened my resolve to remain unemotional. She doesn't know she's chipping away at my wall day by day. I'm used to women seeking me out for money and prestige. No doubt, there have been many who wished to be my wife. Anya doesn't need anything from me but protection, and our marriage provides that for both of us.

I look for her ring finger, and relief springs eternal. She's still wearing it.

"Are you going to the reading of your father's will Monday? We can leave on our honeymoon afterward," I suggest.

"Sure, I bet Mom could use the support."

"How is she?"

"Fine. I speak to her a few times a week. Although I hear you're keeping him busy, Sergei has been there for her and Konstantin."

"A man has to earn his keep."

"Hm." She purses her lips. No doubt she's wondering what she'll be asked to do other than suck my cock and push out a few heirs. I can see why this might not be her dream considering her desire to make her way in the world. I'm still trying to figure out how we'll be able to navigate both our careers.

I watch her add a touch of cream and sip her hot tea. She takes small bites of food and doesn't finish her ham.

"You need to eat, Anya."

"I need to fit in my dress Sunday." She hasn't met my eyes. I'm sure it's her way of punishing me for my coldness earlier, and I deserve it. My heart sinks. I can tell she's unhappy when the light is gone in her eyes, and her cheeks lack color.

Pavel senses the arctic freeze in the room and excuses himself.

"What can I do to make it up to you?" I lean over the table, putting my hand over hers even though she has a fork in it.

"I shouldn't have to tell you," she grumbles under her breath as she takes another sip of tea.

She's right. I know I'm moody and too blunt.

Hazel slips out of the kitchen as if on cue.

I check the time on my watch, a timepiece worth more than most cars driven in London. "I have to go." I lean down and kiss her lips. She resists engaging her own. "I'm sorry. Please give me another chance." I lay my hand over hers as it rests on the tabletop.

"I'll consider it. However, you're using up your allotted requests. I can't wait to meet your brothers. Should I serve something special?" She's warmer to my siblings than she is to me, and the sting of my gruffness is my undoing.

"Not at all. I appreciate the offer," I reply as she pulls her hand from mine.

I grab my jacket and head to the door.

Would it kill me to be nice for a change? Old dogs need time to learn new tricks. I'm set in my ways, and I'm at a loss for how to keep my emotions in check. Hot, deep feelings leave me thinking of her all day and all night. I'm drowning in Anya, and in my battle to survive it, I'm lashing out when she deserves better. Dad always said we must always make decisions based on the good of the Bratva.

Is it better to love and risk losing or to lose her because I won't admit I'm in love?

CHAPTER 20

ANYA

I want to make the mansion pretty and impress Nikolay's family. I have Alex drive me to a local shop to buy fresh flowers. Considering the size of the estates around us, it takes more than twenty minutes. When we get back, Hazel helps me cut the ends off the stems and put them in various vases decorating each room. I should put black roses, or a crow, in Nikolay's bedroom. Instead, I find some white daisies with orange middles and add purple Russian sage to the mix. They go well with his dark furniture and will brighten the room.

I wonder if he remembers our meeting as kids. He was my first crush, even though we were young, I do remember. He has the same eyes, but he was more carefree then. It must be the weight of being thrown into the Bratva unexpectedly and the source of the creases on his forehead.

I thought he hated me when we were kids. It wasn't until Mom told me boys tease you when they like you, and that made his attention less annoying. She was right, it turns out. Teasing is the universal language of a boy trying to get a girl's attention. But now? I'm sure he must feel our chemistry. The trip to Paris was thoughtful and an incredible surprise. Followed by the presence of the ring, and I so love bling! I'm a simple girl at heart, but the sparkles constantly draw my eyes to it. I twist it around my finger all day long, afraid I'll lose it. I'm sure he picked it so I could fit in with women in high society. The class system is alive and well. Granted, those on the bottom are not as bad off as they used to be, but there is a hierarchy in society, and I doubt either will ever go away in my lifetime.

I search the house for tea lights and holders to place lavender-scented candles strategically around the house. I help Hazel set the table and put tapered candles in Waterford crystal holders. His mother must have picked out everything here. She has excellent taste, and I wonder what she's like. Nikolay doesn't talk about his father much. It seems we've both buried our grief to carry out a wedding. I'd like to know what happened. Will he show the real Nikolay to me? Pillow talk is limited to sexual wants and desires, as he drives me crazy with pleasure.

It's late afternoon when the front door opens, and a commotion erupts. Two men stumble in with a few more behind them. I can tell right away who Nikolay's brothers are and hurry to greet them. I tug at my blouse to ensure my navel is appropriately covered, my jeans are clean with a few trendy holes, and my TOMS Parker sneakers are new. Nikolay insisted I order them, saying they were all the rage. I admit he's quite the fashionista where I'm concerned. He says it's because he knows what looks best on me, and I wonder how he can discern that; we've only been reacquainted for a week.

"Wow, you are a sight to behold," one brother says as he pulls me into a bear hug. "I'm Roman; you're going to be my sister-in-law." He's the baby of the family, Nikolay briefed me earlier.

"I guess that's true." I'm caught by surprise and can't resist giggling as my hands grab his shoulders to steady myself. Apparently, the rest of the family isn't as cold as Nikolay.

"Put her down, Roman." Nikolay's gruff voice makes everyone freeze. When did he get home?

"Sorry, brother, no harm done. See?" He places me gently on my feet and turns to embrace Nikolay in a Bratva hug, I assume.

"It's my turn." The brother with longer hair steps forward and gives me a civilized hug. "I'm Dmitry. Welcome to the family."

Dmitry strikes me as the more serious of the two. Roman seems boisterous, but Nikolay told me he's usually introverted. Dmitry is the numbers guy and has a calculating eye. His eye is hyper-focused on the messy bun I quickly threw together earlier and haven't had time to fix. I'm trying not to feel judged as I nervously tuck wisps of hair behind my ear.

"Thank you. I'm so happy you're here, come in," I instruct them as I lead the way into the formal living room. "I suspect you're thirsty. I have a bit of everything in the liquor cabinet. Or tea, if you prefer."

"Vodka," Roman declares. I catch Nikolay's glare as he walks past me to the bar, suddenly becoming a dutiful host. Clearly, he was jealous of Roman touching me. I find this refreshing. He's jealous, a tell-tale sign he has feelings under his rough exterior and passive-aggressive behavior.

Dmitry is dressed in jeans, but they look expensive. His boots remind me of the military. When he removes his leather jacket and rolls up his sleeves, I can't miss the tattoos on his arms. There are too many to discern their meaning. The ink used to mark time served in prison is no longer a statement, but nowadays, tattoos are commonplace, so it's anyone's guess.

Roman has short hair and high cheekbones like his brothers, but his jaw is softer and rounded. He must take after his mother. They're all handsome, and each speaks Russian to Nikolay, no doubt catching up quickly. They clink their shots of vodka, toss it back, and have another round. They are boisterous, but it doesn't bother my fiancé. I relax, knowing I won't take the brunt of his mood tonight. He nods for me to join them and hands me a shot of vodka so I can toast to our upcoming nuptials.

After I slug down the liquor, I excuse myself to check on Hazel and dinner. We're having lamb and potatoes roasted in rosemary. The house is filled with people like it's a holiday, and I'm happy. I welcome his family as if they are my own. They appear to approve of me. I barely remember much about them when we lived in the same town.

By the time dinner is served, the men are in dire need of sobering up. The meal goes off without a hitch, and conversation flies as the guys ask me questions and tell stories about Nikolay, intent on embarrassing him. Nikolay takes it in stride. After a while, I'm exhausted and excuse myself for bed. It's not likely his brothers will be turning in any time soon.

Nikolay stands with me and slips his hand around my arm.

"Good night, Anya, thank you for making tonight special."

"No problem, they're sweet." I glance up and see the smoldering desire in his eyes. Is it possible I've pleased him, and there won't be a slight thrown my way?

"I love them. We're family." His lips are close to mine. I pause, not wanting to break the spell. My feet become cement blocks as I yearn for him to kiss me.

He stands still as if he's debating what to do. I reach a hand up to caress the side of his face. I like seeing him this way, approachable, human, and maybe even vulnerable.

His lips cover mine at long last. I kiss him back, letting him know all is forgiven about this morning. My lips become bruised and swollen under the force of him marking his territory. By the time he pulls away, my panties are damp.

"Good night," I murmur as I go to my room. I'm sure his brothers are aware of our sleeping arrangement, and it wouldn't be remiss for us to have separate rooms before the wedding.

I undress, shower, and throw on a tank top and short bottoms before climbing into bed. It's a tall bed like those in luxury hotels with fluffy pillows and a duvet. I chuckle as I contemplate getting a head start with a jog to spring into it every night.

I lie in the darkness, my windows open, their vibrant voices floating to my window from the patio below. After an hour, their voices fade as they wander into the backyard to smoke cigars and swill more vodka. The distant murmurs of their voices lull me to sleep.

* * *

I'm up early as the house is alive with Nikolay and his brothers. It brings to mind children we might have one day and it makes me happy knowing they will fill this mansion with laughter. It has over twelve rooms counting bathrooms, so it's not an issue putting his family up for a few nights if they choose to stay over. I want them to. Secretly I want to learn more about Nikolay, and his brothers are the perfect source. I enjoy the noise because growing up with my sister, we didn't have other siblings to fight or laugh with. We stuck together out of loving neglect, but it was always the two of us, as Mum wasn't the type to play games with us. I swear her TV was her world.

* * *

"There she is," Dmitry announces my arrival in the dining room. Hazel has a full spread of sausage, eggs, and biscuits. I take a seat next to Nikolay.

"Good morning. I trust you all slept well." I take in Roman, as he's perfectly at ease. He's the type who sticks out in a crowd, he's so serious, and his natural stature is more militant than civilian.

"As well as can be expected without a woman under me," Roman teases.

"So, you're the wild one," I tease back.

"Some say that. I guess we all take our turn. What about you?"

"I'm boring." I pour my tea and add a touch of cream as Hazel makes a plate for me.

"We heard about you being drugged at the bar. That is not boring, my dear sister," Roman reminds me.

He called me sister, and it touched my heart. I'm beginning to feel like I belong with this Bratva family, and after years of being an outsider, it's comforting. I warn myself not to get attached; if Nikolay leaves me, I'll lose them all.

"It was a weird event, for sure."

"You need to be careful. You two have a target on your back, and we're still hoping to find the person who did that to you."

Shivers run up my spine as I picture what they might have done to me. Russians are ruthless when it comes to torture. They are known to be animals, or worse, to get what they want. Failure means death.

"Any word on finding who was behind it?" I haven't had an update in some time.

"I'm tracking her banking transactions in the hopes of finding something. I'm a resident hacker and can navigate the dark web. If she's left a digital footprint, I'll find it." Dmitry nods, convincing me he's dedicated to my safety and making sure Darci never sees the light of day.

I feel for her. Maybe she didn't want to harm me. She might have been coerced into it. I had no way of knowing she wasn't from a famous father. Now, I wonder if her father might be a relative of another mafia family.

"You know, she said her father was famous in rock music. What if he was famous in the criminal world? Could she be a daughter or granddaughter of one of our rivals? They say when you lie, don't stray far from the truth."

"That's a good point." Nikolay studies me with respect. "We know someone was going to exploit our fathers' deaths. What mafia family has the most to gain? Konstantin mentioned the Irish are encroaching on the horse track, one brigadier is light on collections, but it could be skimmed. We're having him and his men watched. Darci could be an Irish name; she doesn't even have to be related. She could have been duped in a number of ways. It makes the entire situation more chaotic." Nikolay scoots forward in his chair and places his hands on the table, interlacing his fingers as he speaks.

"Good point," Roman agrees. "Maybe I should follow Konstantin around, check out the docks, and kick in some doors. Whoever is behind this might also be responsible for papa's death."

"I have my men on it," Nikolay adds matter-of-factly.

"Both murders could be a coincidence. I did find Igor was in a controversial meeting at the oil company. Papa probably helped him launder funds through offshore accounts belonging to larger oligarchs," Dmitry adds. "There is a hierarchy, and everyone is guilty until proven innocent."

I'm trying to comprehend the resources this family has at their fingertips. It's a bird's eye view of how Papa's world was intricately layered, and I wouldn't be surprised if Dmitry didn't know what I had for dinner last week. I also wonder if my computer and phone have trackers on them. Do I have any freedom at all? Or is it only an illusion for not only me but the world? CCTV captures a person's image on average 300 times a day; I researched it. Hearing about the resources sitting at the table, finding Papa's killer isn't as impossible as the police would have us believe.

"I think my fiancée has heard enough. We'll talk later," Nikolay interjects.

"Ready for the big day?" Dmitry inquires to change the subject, but he's sincere, and even though he's a criminal, I'm touched he cares about our wedding plans. He, too, has sensitive dark eyes like Nikolay, but I don't know if my future husband will embrace our union with time or keep his heart in a vault. After Paris, I thought our sleeping arrangements might change, and the disappointment cut like a knife when he kept to the status quo.

"As much as I can be. Today is the final day to pick up things we might have forgotten."

"Who is going with you?" Nikolay quizzes me.

"Alex, of course."

Nikolay seems to agree with this and nods as his fingers wrap around his teacup, and Hazel refills it.

From the look on her face, she enjoys having the men here. I forget she knew them when they were boys, so this is like a homecoming for her. I sit back and enjoy her serving them more like a mother than a servant.

"You'll make a beautiful bride, and we were afraid you'd…" Roman's words are cut off when Dmitry jabs him in the ribs with his elbow.

"Ouch, what the fuck?" he exclaims.

"Manners, brothers," Nikolay warns.

They thought I'd be homely.

I excuse myself and grab my purse for a day out.

Alex is driving, and my mind is elsewhere when my ears fill with the sickening crunch of metal, and the car begins to spin. My head is foggy, feeling like I just came off a wall-banger of a rollercoaster. I'm still struggling to get my bearings when men wearing ski masks pull me from the wreckage.

I look for Alex and see his face bleeding and resting on the airbag; he's unconscious. I can't be taken. Nikolay can't give up bargaining power to get me back. It's like dealing with terrorists. They will always want more. I fight my captors, hitting and kicking but to no avail. One of them jabs me in the shoulder with a needle, and my world turns dark.

CHAPTER 21

avel receives a call. The erratic voice on the other end of the phone is my cue hell is about to rain on someone. The only question is, who?

Pavel hangs up the phone. "The vehicle Alex was driving was hit. It was a pit maneuver done by professionals. Alex is en route to the hospital. Anya is missing."

"Fuck," I yell, grabbing the empty teapot and throwing it against a wall, where it shatters into ceramic splinters. "How could this happen?"

Hazel jumps and moves to sit in the nook opposite Dimity. The mess on the floor is the least of our problems, and we ignore it.

"What we need to do is focus on finding Anya as quickly as possible," Dmitry suggests before shoving a sausage in his mouth. He knows we're on a mission and won't stop until we find her. It might be the last bite of food he gets all day.

"Where is her mother, Inessa? Kateryna? Is Sergei with them?" I fire questions as my mind races. The family needs to be secured in a safe house. I have many homes around the world bought through shell companies.

I chastise myself for not keeping everyone secluded until the wedding. My instincts told me we weren't out of danger. Whoever is behind this didn't have the guts to come at me. Only a coward would take a helpless woman. I've failed Anya. As long as she's missing, the wedding is off, and the Bratva is jeopardized.

"Someone will pay with their life," I swear.

"We're with you, brother," Roman pledges.

I nod, then rake my fingers through my hair. Paris is for lovers, but I didn't need to go there to learn my heart beats faster when I think of Anya. Her touch sets my skin on fire with desire, and I long to see her again. The feelings I had as a teen have exploded since seeing her again. I could have been nicer to her, but if I were, she would see it, and so would the men. How did Papa balance loving Mum and ruling the Bratva? We're trained to stay on the mission, and now, I need to find my bride before another move is made against me.

Hazel looks like she's in shock, so Dmitry lays a comforting hand on her back. "We'll find her," he assures her calmly. We grew up with Hazel and spent holidays here. She was a second mother to us and genuinely fond of Anya.

I have doubts we'll find Anya quickly because the kidnappers will hide her and use her to barter for me. I can't be put to the test because I love her, and I'll have to choose the Bratva. Otherwise, I will not have earned my place as the pakhan.

Dmitry's eyes are on me, waiting for an order, and I don't know where to begin. I can't snap out of my shock. I refuse to accept the fact I might lose someone else I love. I thought not loving Anya would keep her safe, and it was an oversight on my part. Have I loved her all these years? She was my first infatuation, but why is it no other woman can make my cock explode twice in one go?

"Leading looks like fun, and you have all the perks money brings, but you have the weight of the world on your shoulders, and it never goes away," Papa warned. His words haunt me in this moment of weakness. I wonder if he ever had the fear gripping his heart and gut at the same time. Did he fear for Mama's life or ours? If it occurred, he never told me. He was my father, but also my mentor, the one person I went to for serious advice because he could separate his emotions, unlike my brothers, who enjoy life without my responsibilities; Papa and I had grown close in the past few years, so it boggles my mind why he withheld the details of his promise to Igor. Looking back, there might have been references to marrying to make our alliances stronger, and as a bachelor, it was easy to gloss over it, delaying the inevitable.

I would have avenged my father's death if it weren't tied to Igor's. Clearly, the two men were selected for a reason. Their demise wasn't by the hand of rivals; rivals I would have killed without a second thought. My experience is knowing who is in the hierarchy because some men have immunity. There are others we don't want to disturb, and I have to know the difference. The world is filled with powerful men. Making wrong decisions will lead to a blood-bath—our blood. Our world is where men finesse by power, deceit, or fear.

Death squads are dedicated to killing anyone on a list; unfortunately, Papa and Igor were on it. We never know who rats us out. It's like Game of Thrones, political figures have informants every-where, and sadly, Russian citizens inform on their family members.

It's impossible to know what events doomed two leaders in the Bratva. It could have been a heated debate over oil, the ruble exchange rate, or something more pervasive or innocuous as offending an official's wife. If I were a gambling man, I'd say the government was targeting Papa and Igor to make a public example of them. The message is to stay in line, keep your mouth shut, or face the same consequences. The death squad doesn't take hostages. We're used to this in Russia.

"Why now? If Anya or I were targets, why today?" I ask more of myself than others in the room.

"Your wedding, brother. It has to be. We're all here. We could all be a target. Someone wants to take our Bratva," Dmitry sternly replies.

"The house is being fortified with guards. Dmitry, do you have the camera feed from the car accident?"

"I'm working on it." He continues to tap away on his laptop. "Well, they wore masks. It appears Anya was sedated."

I fly to the table and peer at the footage from the government's cameras. "We need to find out if they are Russian."

Pavel chimes in, "How else would someone take over from within if everyone is loyal? They would have to go to an outside source. We have money missing. Money buys mercenaries, or maybe they are in bed with the Irish?"

"What do you mean?"

"The Irish have been making subtle hits near the horse track."

"Gracie!" I worry for my gorgeous white racehorse whom I love. I dial the trainer, who confirms what I already know. Gracie is missing from the paddock.

"How can a horse go missing? Suspects on cameras somewhere!"

"Fuck," Pavel exclaims; he had high hopes for the horse this summer. "The Irish want the racetrack. I assume they are hitting us on two fronts. Does this mean Sergei is working with them?"

I didn't do enough to keep Anya safe. I'm responsible if she's hurt. I push the dark thoughts from my mind, but my fears play like a horror movie in the background. What if she's raped? Assaulted? Cut?

I pace the kitchen; no one can console me.

"I need answers! Now! Every minute counts."

I can't lose Anya. I just found her again after so many years. We haven't had enough time together. I want so much more. I've been an ass, pushing her away to distance myself from the undeniable emotions which can only be love. I can't wait to see her. I'm jealous of any man who looks at her with lust in his eyes, even though I want everyone to appreciate her beauty.

She's the woman who brought happiness back into my life after my father's death. Her positive energy brings light into this otherwise sterile house. The flowers on the kitchen table remind me how thoughtful she is, making my home, our home. She adds more to this house than the expensive modern artwork on the walls. Everything I've done in my life is for a reason. Now, logic be damned. I will turn over every stone until Anya is safely in my arms again.

* * *

"Inessa, I'm asking you again, where is Sergei?" I loom over her. I would strike her,* but I have a rule not to harm innocent women. Is she innocent? I wonder. She's too daft to scheme with the Irish or Sergei.

"I don't know." She wrings her hands in her lap as she sits before me. My men are tossing her house for clues. Other soldiers are searching Sergei's flat as we mess around with her, trying to get details we hope will lead us to Anya before she's hurt.

"Katerynia!" I bark. "What do you know of Sergei?" Anya's sister cringes as I grab her arm, ready to throttle her. "Your sister is being held somewhere. If we don't find her, she'll be killed. Sergei worked for your family for years. Don't leave out any details."

Her eyes grow wide, thinking I might strike her, and if she doesn't speak in the next three seconds, I will. Right now, I'm a stick of dynamite with a short fuse.

"He-he… likes to eavesdrop on our conversations. He's not as professional as the other guards. I let it slip you guys were getting married this Sunday." She closes her eyelids, bracing for retaliation.

"Why was he allowed to be so lax?"

"I don't know. We were more like family in a way. Papa always defended him to Konstantin."

My eyes flare and fixate on Inessa. She's a simpering woman without a spine. "What do you know? Speak, now."

I'm about to grab and shake her by the shoulders when she blurts out, "Sergei is Igor's illegitimate son. No one knew. He has a different last name. I knew he was upset over his father's death, but he's not been himself. We gave him a flat, money, and things to make him happy because I forbade Igor from claiming him. I didn't want to be humiliated. He always went through his paycheck and the allowance Igor gave him," she continues. "I wanted it to stop, cut him off, and make him return to Russia, but he was the son Igor wanted and overlooked his weaknesses. I thought he wanted to fit in with us, but we were buying his silence." Her head dips in shame. "I couldn't say anything. I want my daughter back." She sniffles as tears roll down her face. "I didn't know he could be dangerous. He liked the girls. I thought he had a soft spot for Anya."

"He did," Katerynia adds. "Anya had a crush on him as a teenager, and I thought it was weird how he always knew what we were up to when we'd sneak out of the house and stay up late. It's as if he read our minds; now I think he might have planted bugs in the house." She stirs in her chair. "I mean, he debugs the house. Who's to say he didn't plant his own?"

"Fuck," I shout as I grab the nearest object, a lamp, and send it into a wall, where it shatters. It's symbolic of my life. It's in pieces. Without Anya… I run my hand through my hair. I can't lose her; I just found her again. I'm not ready for it to end.

"The will is to be read after your wedding, but you should know Igor left the business to Anya. That's why she has to marry you. I guess his delusions about his son grew old, and I made sure that was the last official will. I can't live with that man controlling us for the rest of our lives." Inessa wipes the tears off her face with her hand and sniffles. "I want my daughter. Please bring her home," she pleads as our eyes meet. We both lament what might occur, but I toss that mindset away. I will find her.

Pavel and I exchange looks. The family has a few skeletons in their closet, and Anya is paying for it.

I turn to Igor's advisor. "Do you think he'll force her to marry him, or will he hold her hostage to bait me?"

"Tough call," Konstantin replies, silently waiting for my interrogation to finish. "I had no idea. I knew he was being paid money. I assumed he was doing extra jobs for Igor; it was a touchy subject, and I couldn't pressure him too much. I should have put it together."

"Now that I've spoken, they can't be married here. It's illegal," Inessa adds.

"It doesn't matter. Where would he be with her? You know the other holdings, and I assume some might be off the grid."

"There are." He nods once in agreement.

"We need to hit them all; let's go," I reply.

Pavel is already on the phone as we walk to our black SUV. His eyes are lifeless as he explains, "Sergei left a few hours ago, and his phone isn't going through. Fuck. We were sitting ducks. Do you think he killed Igor?"

"Doubtful, he doesn't impress me as a man capable of that. He wanted his love and recognition. With him dead, any shot of it dies with him. This Irish bloke, Cillian, he's the one who heads the Irish mafia. We need Dmitry informed."

Pavel dispatches more soldiers to Inessa's house to provide more security.

I'm angry enough to tear someone's head off. There's no way Pavel could have known about Sergei, we didn't vet him, and Russian records can be changed for a price.

"Igor's death left him perfectly positioned to take over with the help of others," I murmur.

Pavel runs his hand over his stern chin. "Sergei needs someone to help him. Who do we suspect?"

"The Irish are helping him," I exclaim. "It makes sense because Gracie is missing, and we've heard rumblings the Irish are muscling in on our betting outlets. That's George's territory, so either he's in on it or being played. Someone is skimming money to finance a takeover. It's all falling into place."

* * *

We return to my estate and inform my brothers. Hazel is making meat pies for us to take on the road.

"I'm here for you, brother," Roman says while checking his gun to make sure it's loaded. "We're going to need more weapons and hit some of their cash houses and stir shit up."

"Basement. Papa was always ready for a war." The room falls silent for a second as his memory hangs over us. I've pushed down my anger over his death. "I don't think Sergei is capable of killing Papa and Igor; it's a reach. He's not that bright, he's flashy, but there's no telling what he knew of Igor or the will."

"I'll get all the men to beef up patrol on the house; the others will mobilize at a secure location. I'll send them to a place we've never used, so if someone is compromised, we'll know we have a mole," Pavel says. "Others are going to create chaos on the opposite end of town once we have the details on the location."

"Smart thinking. Get on it. Dmitry, anything yet?"

Pavel dispatches men to check all our vehicles, with more men arriving to help guard the house and follow us when we have a list of places to check.

Hazel sits, and I pour her tea; she's distraught over Anya.

"I'll find her, Hazel," I assure her, even though I have no clue how.

Anya must be scared. "Where could Sergei take her? I want answers. Now! Konstantin, you knew him best. Let's look at your suggestions first."

Finally, my head has cleared, and I'm in military mode. War has been declared, and I must fight to keep what's mine.

My heart grows heavier with each passing second. Seconds become minutes, and it's all in slow motion. The idea that someone could snatch Anya from under my nose is unbelievable. We're all capable of guerrilla tactics to get what we want. We're ruthless, too. This is what concerns me the most.

"Roman, what will Sergei do to her?"

He shrugs. "He wants the throne. What would you do for it?" His eyebrows furrow, and his jaw tightens. Really? He chooses now to give it to me straight rather than sugarcoat his bad news.

CHAPTER 22

ANYA

I have a splitting headache, and my first thought is I didn't drink anything this time. What the fuck is going on? I open my eyes and squint into what looks like a noonday sun filtering through a small dirty window. The musty smell of corn chips and mothballs hangs in the stale air. Thank goodness it's not summertime temperatures, or I'd be sweating.

A chair scrapes and a familiar voice is talking on a phone. "Hit them, Cillian. I gave you the horse as a down payment. As soon as I wed Anya, it's all mine. You won't be sorry." He clicks off and turns to me.

"Ah, you're up at last." Sergei is the last person I expected to see here. He flips his sunglasses on his head and takes two long strides to reach me.

My wrists and ankles are numb from sitting in one position for too long. "Water," I eke out.

"Water? Aren't you surprised? I'm not to be toyed with, Anya. I thought we had something going when you were younger." He nods to another man in the room, who steps out of the shadows with an automatic machine gun slung over his shoulder. The man grabs a tumbler off the washing machine and fills it with water from the laundry sink faucet. He lifts the cup to my parched lips. I drink until the container is empty, gulping water to wash the sedative out of my system. I slept and didn't hallucinate, so I'm less fearful of the side effects.

"I was a kid, Sergei. What did you want from me?"

"It was college; you got to see other men, and I wasn't good enough. You moved out," he sneers.

"I grew up. What did you expect?" He's not the Sergei I knew. He's changed. His eyes are cold and void of emotion. It's as if I'm looking at a stranger.

"I want you. I've always wanted you. Father had no idea I loved you."

"Father?"

"Yes, we share a father. It was the best-kept secret. Even your mother kept it to herself. When Igor died, I used it to my advantage to claim the Bratva with you by my side."

It takes me a minute to understand what he's saying. If he's Papa's illegitimate son, that makes him my half-brother. Has he gone mad?

"Sergei, if you let me go back to Nikolay, I'm sure we can work this out." I put on my most sincere face and try to spin the situation, given that I'm helpless and the guard in the room doesn't look Russian. Double fuck. I doubt he'll care about me or what is right in this situation, given the fact he was probably the one who pulled me from the vehicle. "What happened to Alex?"

"It's my understanding he's still alive. However, the Volkov brothers will be taken out once they step off their estate." He paces the cement floor in black jeans and a long-sleeved T-shirt; a filled gun clip is on his waist.

Papa said he was a good shot, serving time in the Russian army before he joined us in London. I assume he has tactical training, and there is no way for me to warn Nikolay.

"What of my mum? Kateryina? Are they okay?"

"They are home, no doubt being interrogated. It's pointless. No one will find us. We're in the Irish's black site. There's no way they will look for us here."

Finally, a clue. Nikolay and Pavel suspected the Irish were moving into the racetrack, and I pray they put it together.

"So, you needed the help of the Irish to do this? They will own you, Sergei."

He lets out a haughty chuckle, chills run up my spine. He's gone mad.

I long to see Nikolay, not because I need him to rescue me again, but because I love him. Deep down inside, we have a connection. The stress of this situation stirred memories of us as kids. He promised me then that he would marry me and kissed my cheek. Not long after, my family moved away. Our fathers had dealings, but us kids never saw each other after I moved.

"Father left the Bratva to you, so once I kill Nikolay, I'll take over. It will all be mine. I'm the rightful heir!" he exclaims like a madman. I noticed him acting differently after Papa died, but there is no way I could have predicted he'd gone mental in his delusions.

I wondered why Papa kept him on as a guard when he didn't always behave professionally. A guard needs to keep his feelings in check and remain professional to not be compromised. Was Sergei treated more like a family member? Perhaps, and I wonder if he's capable of killing.

"What of Baran? Did you hurt him?"

"Baran is a better fighter than I am, but someone else did it and killed Father, which left my future open to having everything. All the Irish want is the racetrack."

"They will never let you go, Sergei, don't you see? You are better off giving yourself up."

He slaps me, hard, on my cheek and the chair I'm tied to rocks. Fuck. That hurt, but I bite my lip and refuse to cry out in pain.

"Learn your place; you're only worth something until the Bratva becomes mine. Then I can treat you however I want. You'll be powerless to stop me."

Fuck, I'm stuck in a basement with a madman, and I'm being used as bait. I pray Nikolay finds me. But what are the odds of that? Slim. I've decided the raw facts are more helpful, meaning I need to get myself out of here.

Sergei has a holster on his belt, but the huge guard is another sticky situation. I can't go up against them both.

The missing horse will tip off Nikolay. I wonder what Katerynia knows. I'm sure they've been questioned, as Sergei isn't at work today. Even if he made an excuse, it's too much of a coincidence I'm missing, and he's nowhere to be seen. Throw in Nikolay's horse, and it's a trifecta.

"What, do you think Nikolay will save you? Wake up, Anya, he's never going to love you. You can be free of this life once you sign everything over to me." He paces back and forth as he keeps an eye on me. "I'm the Petrov son and rightful heir. And the Bratva will know the truth once and for all," he sneers, and I use his going off the rails to twist my wrists to see if I can free my hands.

Obviously, they tossed my cell phone and are using burners. There's no end to the money I would pay to see Nikolay again. I know we were destined to be. I don't know why it took me so long to piece it together. We were kids. I didn't take him seriously, thinking he was young, and I thought I was a passing thought. I wonder if he remembers his promise to marry me. I will willingly wed him. I need to break free one more time. I have to tell him I remember it all now, and I love him.

CHAPTER 23

NIKOLAY

Two cops knock at the door and hand me Anya's purse and cell phone found at the crash scene. Pavel listens to them. I'm too distraught to hear the details, none of which matters. Anya is gone. We file a missing person's report but know it will be useless, and we can't say much. They know she's missing, so we can't deny it, but we'll handle this alone.

I hold her belongings, and the small, broken box in her handbag tumbles out. The purse is one we picked out together.

I return to the kitchen, contemplating the box. It's not the one I gave her, but it's too small. I open the crushed lid and inside are gold cufflinks engraved with our initials. Strangely, I never saw a charge from the jeweler on her credit card statement. It's a thoughtful gift she paid for herself, which means she cares for me. I stuff the cufflinks in the front pocket of my jeans, hoping they will bring me good luck.

I long to tell her no woman has ever been good enough for me because my heart has belonged to her since we were kids. If we had never reunited, I would have ended up in a boring, loveless marriage, and she would probably bury herself in school and work.

I have to find her. Even if she weren't connected to the Bratva, she would be my choice for a wife. Now, sorrow creeps into my chest like a cold, dense fog, knowing I may never get to tell her I love her. I can't admit defeat. There is still time, and I'll never give up.

"Dmitry, you need to find Cillian. I'm sure Sergei has her well hidden. We'll hit the three obvious locations Konstantin knows about. We need to lean on the Irish and George. I'm sure he must have his ear to the pavement. What does he know that we don't? And can we trust him?"

"On it," he exclaims, draining a can of Red Bull.

"What can I do?" Konstantin asks.

"Who has an in with the Irish? Can I meet with Cillian?"

"Doubtful under the circumstances; he's probably holed up in a safe house. I'd advise against it. We need to be prepared for hits on our businesses. But I'll see what I can do."

"Have a team check out your locations for signs of Anya or men gearing up for war." I turn to Roman. "Get the weapons ready, we're going to hit the places Dmitry finds, and we're going to kick down doors until we find her."

"Sergei should be making demands by now if he wants to prevent the loss of men dying by our bullets. How many men could he have turned?" I ask.

"I say we rough George up. Enough is enough. He had to suspect something. He's been at this too long not to know what's going on." Pavel makes a valid point, and I agree.

"Find George, bring him to our warehouse, and have our men torture him. I'm fucking done with asking questions. I want him to sing like a bird."

Pavel nods and goes outside to give orders to the trusted men waiting for instructions.

My phone rings.

"I know you are amassing an army, but I have Anya, and you have nothing."

"Sergei," I say his name to alert people around me. Dmitri scurries over to his keyboard to track the call.

"You won't find us, so don't bother looking. The Bratva belongs to me. I have Anya. Winner takes all."

"Fuck you. You'll regret the day our paths cross again."

"Good luck. I know everything about you, but you know nothing about me."

He has a point. It pisses me off, but I can't let my emotions get the best of me. I listen for background noise on the call, anything to give me a clue as to where they are, and when I'm about to give up, Sergei pauses, and I hear the Tube.

"Be careful venturing out." Sergei's phone goes dead.

"I heard the Tube; we need to find that train. It will narrow down the search area."

"There are too many, brother." Dmitry scoffs. "I'm great at this, but London is a huge city. Give me your phone. Let's see if he was stupid enough to use a cell tower. If so, I'll track his car and the family's vehicles. We might get lucky, and it will ping from the GPS tracker. Sergei doesn't impress me as being bright. He's flashy and goes off half-cocked to think he can get away with this."

"Wouldn't be the first time stupidity led to an all-out war," I grumble as I hand my phone to Dmitry. He looks at incoming calls and finds the burner number. Sergei didn't use Wi-Fi, and Dmitry runs it through programs on his high-powered laptop.

I hold my breath, hoping he can pull off a miracle. If we can narrow down the area where Sergei might be holding her, we will have more information than we do now. The adrenaline has my heart ticking like a time bomb.

"Okay, I have a cell phone tower. Now I need to triangulate it with the subway at the time he called. He has to be in a densely populated area."

Roman is in the kitchen loading and stacking guns on the counter so he and Pavel can carry them to our vehicles parked out front. From the security feed to the house, Roman observes vehicles amassing in front of the house as more men arrive to help.

"I know London like the back of my hand," Konstantin declares, peering over my brother's shoulder. "I bet Sergei is holed up in the East End, where our Irish rivals work. He's using the Irish, so we need to assume he has some of Cillian's men." He spitballs ideas. His voice is filled with angst and adrenaline. These are the situations we dread, but at the same time, we know they are inevitable.

This bastard stole the love of my life, and I will fucking annihilate him when I find him.

"It's still too big, but I have it narrowed down to a square mile. I'll cross-reference it with property owned by Cillian's corporations," Dimity adds enthusiastically. "We'll find her," he says as his eyes dart as fast as his fingertips fly. God, I never loved technology as much as I do today. "I'm also hacked into the CCTV cameras with facial recognition."

"Fuck, you're incredible." Inside, adrenaline burns in my veins. I hope we're not too late.

"The car is loaded. I say let's head out, and you can direct us from there," Roman suggests. I'm happy my brothers are here to help.

"I'm behind you with a vehicle full of men," Konstantin adds as he gives me a reassuring pat on the back as we file out.

CHAPTER 24

NIKOLAY

*T*wo days before the wedding, my bride was missing. Talk about karma biting me in the ass!

I'm in the front seat as we drive down one alley after another, looking for Sergei's car. Sweat is puddling under the chest protectors we wear over our t-shirts in anticipation of heavy gunfire. I wipe my brow with the back of my hand. I hope the GPS chips are working in all the vehicles he might have used to carry out this stunt, and I pray he was stupid enough to drive one of them to the location where he has Anya.

We hit a pothole, and our butts fly out of the seats. I grip the dashboard even though I'm wearing a seatbelt.

Konstantin calls to say George is talking. He said a huge Russian from Belarus might be helping Sergei. Other than that, he suspects the Irish are involved. He has no clue where the horse is. It would be stupid to kill a valuable asset, but my enemies would not think twice about killing her to piss me off.

"We could handle this for you, Nikolay. That's our job," Pavel states.

"No! It's my war. Anya is mine, and anyone who puts a hand on her is a dead man. I won't rest until we kill them all. The Irish will think twice after this."

Dark clouds gather overhead, reminding me of the afternoon I picked Anya up at her flat. Everything reminds me of her in one way or another. I long to have her in my arms and vow to hold her when we sleep every night for the rest of my life.

"There," Dmitry shouts, "the laptop shows up at a house beside you, but keep driving." My brother's welcome voice comes through the vehicle's Bluetooth as he remains home to oversee our mission.

Pavel passes the house, and my adrenaline surges; my heart is beating so hard it pulsates in my ears. Could it be we're going to find her?

"I'm going in first," Roman calls out, opening his door before Pavel brings the vehicle to a complete stop. We park in an empty driveway three houses away.

"Roman, I'll go first," I say.

"I'm the one who's best at this. I'll take out whoever is in our way and save Sergei for you," he declares as he hands out weapons from the trunk.

"Fine," I acquiesce. He has a valid point. He's worked with the most skilled military men in the world, which is why he's our utility man. I need to let him do what he does best. It's for the good of the family.

"Besides, you have to get married and seal the deal, or it's going to be a long, drawn-out war," Pavel adds.

"Right, no pressure…" I joke, but no one laughs.

We follow military protocol, single file, as we descend upon the dilapidated house on crack row, named for the number of homeless drug addicts.

It's late afternoon, the sun is low, and we're shadowless thanks to the cloud cover. A burst of shots rings in the humid air as Roman makes his approach. There's only one way in, and a bullet whizzes past our heads in the narrow corridor. I'm sure there are plenty of men and plenty of ammo inside. Bullets bounce off buildings and rusted, broken-down cars with a ping. Ricocheting bullets are a legitimate concern and the reason I hate shootouts in tight spaces. We take turns returning fire. We're sitting ducks, and it's every man for himself.

Thankfully, Roman got the men stationed on the rooftop. We duck, take cover, then advance again when Roman gives us the sign. The gravel crunches under our feet as we move. They have us dead to rights. We can't hide during a direct assault.

Roman returns fire like the pro, inserts another clip, and waves his right hand for us to advance. I follow him, weapon drawn, finger on the trigger, as we walk around fallen Irishmen, judging by the Celtic tattoos on their forearms. I'm hoping this is over before the cops arrive.

A unit of men on the other side of town creates a distraction to limit the availability in our area should our mission become exposed. Even with suppressors on our weapons, the site is densely populated. Citizens don't like guns in general; bullets flying by windows are frowned upon. We need to get in and out quickly.

A man is down with a wound in his leg, but he motions us on. I take a hit in my chest, it winds me, but I struggle to stay on my feet and focus on finding Anya. My arm is bleeding; I don't feel much. As long as I can carry my machine gun and the Sig on my belt, I'll walk until I die.

It seems like an eternity before we surround the house. In reality, it probably took less than a minute. Roman uses a small detonator to blow the door, and the noise is deafening. We pause to recover from the blast before we storm the old house. I follow Roman to the basement.

He tosses a flash grenade inside the door we breach. I hate to think of Anya in there with munitions, but it's our only option to stun our opponents.

Smoke fills the air, my ears ring, and we advance. Roman fires at the first man he sees, and I step over the giant Russian who's dead before he hits the ground. The second wave of our attack worked. I squeeze the trigger and kill a man still on the ground and stomp on his chest out of sheer anger as I pass.

George was right, the Russian was one of my disloyal soldiers, just as he described him: large, burly, and without remorse.

My eyes burn as I peer through the smoke and rubble. I make out a figure in a chair ahead of me. Is it my mind playing tricks on me, or is it her? I continue to walk. My chest hurts like a son of a bitch, because my vest caught a second bullet. I trudge on.

Anya! I rejoice because seeing her face means my prayers are answered. She has a cloth shoved in her mouth, her face is dirty and swollen, and her eyes are wide with terror.

I pull a pocket knife from my belt; I cut through her zip ties and remove the gag from her mouth. The confusion in the basement leaves no room for words. No one can hear. It's as if we're underwater, and words are muffled in the commotion.

Sergei steps out of the shadows with a handgun poised on me. To my left, Roman has a gun zeroed in on him. Sergei's face is filled with surprise from the attack, and his crazed eyes meet mine. I pull my revolver and shoot, but not before he gets a round off, hitting my shoulder. Roman fires at him as well.

The dust settles. Sergei is dead. Our adrenaline rush is over. I need air, stitches, and Anya's arms around me. Roman and Anya help me walk, and we clear the old crack house. The sun peeks out from behind a cloud. I take her face in my hands and kiss her, but it's short. We have to move. Our cleaners are here picking up the brass and carrying away our fallen who didn't make it.

Anya holds my hand in the back seat. Her tears fall on my face as I'm slumped in her lap. I'm whisked away to the closest safe house outfitted as an emergency room, where our doctor has been on standby all day.

"I'm fine. It's over," I mumble before I pass out.

* * *

I hear an IV beeping when I come to and wiggle my toes. I can feel them, what a relief. I'm not in my bed. Fuck, that's not a good sign. The lights are dim, yet the most beautiful woman in the world is looking into my eyes. She reassures me I'm going to be okay. I raise a hand to touch her head and pull her lips to mine as I close my eyes and enjoy the sweetest kiss I've ever known.

"I love you, Anya. I have ever since we were kids. I meant what I said then. I'm going to marry you." I grin. Far be it from me not to keep a promise.

Tears stream down her face. "You remembered. I did, too! Your cologne smells like the flowers we walked through. I didn't know you were the boy who pulled my braids and gave me my first kiss until this week."

I nod. "I never forgot you; it was easier to live with you safely out of my reach."

"I love you, Nikolay, but you need to rest," she whispers against my cheek. The warmth of her close to me is the only medicine I need. She changed into clean clothes while I slept, and now she crawls into the hospital bed with me, snuggling under my uninjured arm.

"How bad am I?"

"A few broken ribs, a bullet hole in your shoulder. The doctor said you'll be fine. The ribs will take the longest to heal."

"I'm sure it's not the first time my ribs have been broken. I guess I'll need another tattoo to cover this scar." I nod to my left shoulder.

"I kind of like it. By the way, I found the cufflinks in the pockets of your jeans."

"They made it. I kept them for good luck," I explain.

"They must be." She raises her head, smiles, and kisses me tenderly before she carefully lays her head on my chest as it's bandaged tightly.

"Fuck, my ribs hurt."

"I can move," she suggests.

"Don't you dare think of moving. I want to go home." The pain tells me I'm alive. And for now, it's enough. Life with Anya by my side is all I need.

Fuck, my shoulder burns, and my thoughts drift. I pull Anya to me, comforted by her presence and admission of love. It's as if we're kids again, and the thrill of my first love returns like it was yesterday, only we're grown and about to tie the knot.

CHAPTER 25

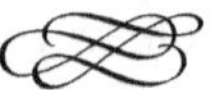

ANYA

A week has passed. We've enjoyed hot evenings of incredible sex combined with Nikolay's shorter workdays. I revel in his arms at night and how he puts on a façade when the men are around like he's not totally in love with me.

Cillian still has his white racehorse, Gracie. It normally wouldn't be tolerated for the Irish to keep it. However, Nikolay 'gave' it to Cillian as a gesture of good faith, hoping he'll be able to keep the peace.

It turns out I'm the Queen of the Petrov Bratva as Dad left everything to me. He said he was proud of me for sticking up for myself and no doubt a law degree will come in handy with the business. He left me to provide for Mum and Katerynia. On a personal level, he even wrote he was sure Nikolay and I would have a long and prosperous life.

"You still want to get married?" Nikolay asks as he caresses my face and we lie in his oversized king bed while the morning sun dances on the walls. "You don't need me. I mean, maybe for protection, but you're a wealthy woman in your own right."

I pause. I never considered how much I love him, and in the course of our whirlwind courtship, I trust him. Getting married and having a career doesn't mean I don't want him to warm my bed at night, and, more importantly, he'll do his best to keep me safe. I fully understand our treacherous world and learned enemies can come at us from any direction, and they don't wear labels like my expensive wardrobe.

"There's no one I want by my side more than you." My eyes soften as I take in his handsome face, and his once icy blue eyes are now as placid as a lake in the summertime with blue skies overhead. I don't know if it's love or the wedding tomorrow, but I'd love to have children with him. I have fallen head over heels in love with this man who will stop at nothing to keep me and our future family safe. The thought of a baby and toddlers running around the secluded estate, mini replicas of us, warms my heart.

"Our marriage will merge our families and empires," he says.

"It's what our fathers wanted. I'm so happy we ditched that oil stock."

We both take a moment to remember our fathers and their ill-fated business decision. Granted, Grigory, Nikolay's father, wasn't heavily involved. We believe it was more of a guilt by association, and he was held accountable for his friend's questionable behavior when the powers that be gave the orders.

We laze around, but the sun is our alarm clock, and guests are arriving.

"I wish we had time to make love," Nikolay says as he nips one of my nipples between his fingers.

"Not like we weren't up all night. I mean, my girlie parts are still recovering." I snicker.

"Just the way I want it. I don't want to be far from your thoughts, ever."

Like I could ever forget him; we've known each other our entire lives, and fate brought us back together.

He is generous with his kisses, and our lips meet. I snake my hands around his neck.

"Damn it, if we continue, my brothers will be waiting for a long time, and idle time is the work of the devil, especially with Roman," he whispers as he rolls off me with a groan.

He stands, and his boner is ready for action.

"Maybe a quickie?" I tease him.

He turns, and a wide grin graces his once broody face. "You read my mind, you wench." He snickers. "Turn over," he commands.

I prop up on all fours. He pulls me to the side of the bed, and the height is just right for his hard cock. He slips his fingers in me first. "You always taste so sweet," he murmurs before I hear him licking his fingers like I'm the filling of a cherry pie.

"I'm going in hard and fast," he warns.

I brace my arms on the mattress, and his pulsating cock enters me completely, filling my tight pussy as his hand lands in the middle of my back, and my pussy gushes around him. It's so hot when he places a hand on me. It can be as subtle as holding my hand as we walk, holding my neck in one position as he has me pinned against a wall as he takes me into his office, or stroking my body in foreplay.

I want him, all of him. He groans, and my pussy walls tense around him. The friction is giving me chills. I clutch the bedding and gasp for air as wave after wave of incredibly intense orgasms wash over me. I feel him spilling his seed in me. He collapses on my back, holding me to him as if he'll never let me go.

He finally pulls his cock out as he stands, and the warmth of his cum slides down my thighs. I'm filled in every sense of the word.

* * *

Dmitry and Roman join us in Nikolay's favorite living room because he loves hanging out with his brothers and Pavel. They can also crack a window and sneak cigars. I've caught on to the boys' loopholes to no smoking in the house.

It's time for pre-dinner drinks. They open vodka, pouring it for everyone. I know better than to tell Nikolay he shouldn't drink it. I'm sure he's been through worse injuries.

"Thank you, brothers." He raises his glass, and they all tap them and slug the liquid down.

"Mama's coming in tonight," Roman informs us.

"Well, I hope she won't be disappointed we're leaving on a honeymoon after the wedding," Nikolay announces with a devilish glint in his eyes, which means he's looking forward to spanking my ass over the bow of his yacht as we fuck ourselves to death under the moonlight on the French Riviera.

"Not at all. She wants to see you for herself." Roman's eyes dance as he cajoles Nikolay. I understand Roman is the baby in the family, and she loves to fawn over him. Now, it appears she's only concerned with Nikolay's recovery.

"I can't wait," I add, wondering what she's like and if we'll get along.

"Pavel will pick her up. I have an incredible feast prepared," I add as I excuse myself to prepare for her arrival. The house is filled with flowers, and we have a suite prepared for her upstairs with red roses and little mint chocolates on her pillowcase. I hope I didn't overdo it, but we'll be family, and I only have one opportunity to impress her.

* * *

Natasha arrives with the boys all speaking to her at once, laughing and hugging. They smother her with affection. She finally reaches me.

"Anya, it's been years. I'm so excited to see you and Nikolay together at last," she beams. Her face glows as her dark hair cascades down her shoulders, curled so perfectly it swirls like the softest ice cream ever made. She's dressed in a designer pantsuit and wears a long trench coat to accentuate her slim figure and the stature of a woman who was once a model in Europe before the boys were born.

I hug her and greet her in Russian. I kiss both her cheeks, and her designer perfume fills the foyer. She's dressed elegantly, and I'd expect nothing less. She's beautiful.

"Let's move into the solarium," I suggest. "Drinks are served."

"You're a woman after my own heart," she purrs and slides her arm through mine as she leads the way because this was her house for many years and no doubt she enjoyed living here.

"I love what you've done with the house," I compliment her. "Funny how it suits our personalities. Nikolay loves his living room."

"Oh, it was nothing, an early wedding gift. I know you both so well. I occasionally heard from your mother over the years. It's a shame my husband and your father aren't here for your wedding day. I can't change what happened. I'm just relieved you and Nikolay are fine." She pats my arm as if I'm of her blood. "I knew you'd be good for Nikolay. He needs a strong woman at his side, now, tell me about the wedding. I hear your dress is the first of its kind and hasn't been released to the A-listers yet." She gives me an impish grin as she squeezes my arm in excitement, and for a second, I wonder if the dress wasn't obtained under pressing conditions just for me. "Now, we're having the wedding in Paris at the hottest hotel. I can't wait, it's been redone, and we're the first to use it, so we'll be sure to set the record on the most fashionable wedding of the year."

"I'm just happy we can finally get married," I add modestly.

"Oh, my dear, you are the toast of London and Volgograd. Enjoy it. The moments of glory are fleeting in our world. Walk proudly. We both lost a loved one, honor them as you walk down that aisle and enjoy your honeymoon. I can tell by the glow on your face it's already started."

I bow my head; she's so open about everything. Her expensive heels click on the tile, and she still walks like a runway model. I don't know how I can measure up to her grace since I will be the new Queen.

"I'm here for you, for anything," she whispers as she accepts a drink from Roman. Dmitry takes her other arm and rattles on about how he's cracked Interpol, and from there, Roman boasts his sniper skills in the attack leading to my rescue.

By the time we gather around the dinner table, we have the presence of more servants. Now, Hazel can cut back on her hours and do what she loves. She's a chef who enjoys cooking gourmet meals for us and having a small herb garden near her cottage.

Natasha slips into the kitchen after dinner and has a long visit with Hazel over hot tea, and the rest of us retire to the billiards room for drinks and games. We've become a family faster than most, and I'm sure it's because we all know that life is short. Every day, we have to reach out and find the good and the bad in the world, and we need to hope the good wins.

* * *

Nikolay's mother insists I call her 'Mama' and as I'm getting dressed, she enters the room for brides and hands me a long, thin box.

"Open it. It's my pearls. Welcome to the family."

I open the box lined with silk and the most incredible iridescent black pearl necklace in it. My breath catches in my throat.

"They will set your wedding dress off nicely, don't you think?"

"They are lovely, thank you," I murmur as I carefully lift the necklace and hand it to her to clasp it around my neck.

"Wear them; they don't belong in a box." She kisses my cheek. "I'll leave you with your mother and sister to get ready."

"Please, join us," I state. She has no daughters, but she's my family now, and I want to include her.

My mom and sister arrive, and we all chat excitedly as the makeup artist and hair specialist work their magic on me.

My wedding day is the first of June in the most elaborate hotel, the Hotel of Paris, and the view of the Eiffel Tower is magnificent. The rooms are a mix of old-style furniture made with a modern twist, and it captures the vibe of the past and brings it to the present. The beds are high, and the duvets are extremely fluffy, but I doubt we'll notice as they will be tossed to the floor as soon as Nikolai carries me over the threshold.

The church on the street is covered with our men, and over one hundred friends and business associates gather in the pews.

I walk down the aisle. Dmitry gives me away, and he hands me to Nikolay, who carefully pulls his jacket sleeve up to expose the cuff-links I had made for him. Dmitry joins Roman at the altar. Natasha and my sister stand up for me, and Mom is crying in the first pew, dressed in the most expensive dress she's ever worn. She looks fantastic for the first time in her life with a dress tailored for her and her gray hair colored expertly, making her look years younger.

My hair is coiffed in the most incredible hairdo, my French manicure is perfect, and my heart beats so loudly in my ears that I'm surprised no one else hears it. It's bursting with love for the man I have now chosen to be my partner for life and all it entails.

For now, I'm content to say 'I do' to Nikolay, and when we've sealed the deal with a passionate kiss, the church erupts with cheers and clapping. We partake in many pictures, letting selected paparazzi in as it's good for business, and then make our way to the hotel for a formal sit-down dinner.

We only have eyes for each other but must greet all our guests and walk from table to table. I'm introduced to so many couples. The number of names I've heard makes me dizzy.

"Just a few more hours, my love, and then we'll be alone. We fly out tomorrow for the yacht. I can't wait to show you the sights."

I raise a hand to his cheek and tenderly kiss his lips. He still has pain from the ribs, and his arm is not one hundred percent yet, but it doesn't prevent him from holding me tightly in his arms for our first dance.

After others join us on the dance floor, I'm allowed to sit, nibble at food, and have another glass of champagne.

"I hope you'll come to visit me in Russia," Natasha imparts on me as she has a male friend on her arm who is escorting her around.

"I look forward to it," I say, then proceed to hug her. I'm happy to have her as an ally.

"I wouldn't be opposed to the pitter-patter of tiny feet either. Babies bring so much happiness."

Point taken, the informal approval to carry on the Bratva legacy has been passed down by the last matriarch who bore it. The glint of happiness in her eyes after her husband's tragic death makes me want to leap to fulfill her request.

My gown was raved about due to the designer, no doubt, but I squealed with delight when I made the cover of Vogue. I might have the picture framed and on my desk in the loft on the fourth floor overlooking the foyer. I like the view of the entrance for safety, and I have the added benefit whereby I can sneak to the top of the mansion and take in the panoramic view of the countryside.

CHAPTER 26

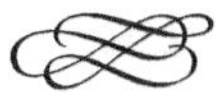

ANYA

*N*ikolay and I walk around naked most of the time on his
yacht named Grace. I never realized it's my name's
meaning in Russian, and now I understand why his racehorse was
particularly special to him. She was Gracie.

He's had the yacht for a few years but never used it much. Sublimi-
nally he was waiting for me. He told me about the sex clubs he used
to frequent and how he was lonely, not knowing he longed for me
all this time. He took my family leaving Russia hard, and as a young
man, he took it personally.

The crew takes care of our every need, and the chef prepares
Michelin-quality food for us. I have no desire to go home as I want
to have Nikolay to myself as long as possible.

"You know, you could work for our company when you graduate."
We're eating eggs Benedict and watching the morning sun dance
on the cerulean water. I'm content, even happy. I commit this

moment to memory. It's perfection. My gorgeous husband not only gave me a wedding I never dreamed of, but also gave me the most intense sexual workouts numerous times a day. He no longer pushes me away but instead seeks to pull me closer at every opportunity, and, as a gift, he's given all his attention to me. From shopping, boating, taking the jet skis out for fun, and jumping the wakes of yachts as they pass, it's been one thrill after another.

"Really? Would I go to prison?" I joke. Is it really a joke?

"Why don't you do written contracts with loopholes only we know how to break if necessary? I bet you would be good at it."

"I can't even strategize chess; I doubt it."

He reaches over the table and takes my hand. "Never underestimate your potential, my love."

His eyes are so serious I can't dissuade him, and I agree to think about it. I have one year to go with an internship. Maybe I can change mine to contractual law and give it a go.

We finish eating and take a dip in the warm Mediterranean Sea under the summer sky. The past four days have been a gift. We both know it will be short-lived.

I dress for dinner in town. We're taken ashore by tender along with a few bodyguards who follow us at a discreet distance. We visit the rooftop at Hotel Paris where we sip Aperol Spritz cocktails and look out at the sea.

"Are you trying to get me tipsy? You know I'm a sure thing," I tease Nikolay as I cozy up to him and take in the sun's fading light shimmering on the water.

"Mm, nothing is too good for my woman. But I'm here to make sure you're safe. I never want you to feel like you need to sneak out of the house again."

"Mm. I learned my lesson if it's any consolation."

"I'll take it, but I never want to go through that again," he kisses my forehead. "You look gorgeous in that sundress, but I'd rather stare at you without it." His voice deepens, and I'm beginning to think the man is insatiable.

"Let's finish these drinks and make love on the beach."

"It comes with a fine if caught."

"We can afford it. Besides, we have bodyguards to run interference," I reply, deciding the guards can be useful.

He snickers and nods. "I see you catch on quickly, my love."

"Mm," I purr as I finish my drink and suggestively run my tongue over my lips.

"You do know that turns me on," he says, pulling me into a tight embrace.

"Maybe…" His lips descend upon mine. I melt into him. He owns me, body and soul.

His phone vibrates in his pocket, and I groan.

"Yes, well, I planned on Dmitry going to New York to oversee the deal. If shit is going to occur, I want him there to represent our interest and to help our Bratva brother."

"Please tell me we can still have sex on the beach," I moan.

"Yes." He flicks the tip of my nose with his fingertip. "But we must head back tomorrow. I have some big deals, and the world doesn't stop because we're on our honeymoon."

"What the hell, I thought you ruled the world," I tease.

"Well, it goes on without me, but sometimes, it's better with me in it," is his gruff reply before he kisses me deeply. I'm not wearing panties, and my wetness fills my womanly opening. It will only be a matter of time before my dress has a wet spot.

"I think we need to find that beach. Now."

* * *

We had to cut the honeymoon short. Nikolay wanted to see Dmitry before he left for New York to oversee a huge cocaine shipment. It appears we're in bed with a Russian group there, and Dmitry's friend, Kirill, is his contact. Cocaine's popularity is on the rise in Europe, and it's as if the '80s have reemerged. The cost is dictated by the price of importing it from South America, and law enforcement has caught on to our ways of smuggling.

Over time, I've become more involved with the business. It's my legacy. I won't give orders to take lives, but I enjoy coming up with new ideas for legitimate business ventures. It appears it's my niche.

I loved the bridal store, and by investing money in it, we've been able to open another location. I have my hands full helping Nikolay expand our empire. My last year of law school starts soon. I'll finish my degree, but I haven't decided how I will use it. I have my own money, but Nikolay insists on paying for everything. He plans weekend getaways for us to enjoy culinary delights from around the world as we take pictures of the scenery of our neighboring European countries. Our plan is to travel as much as we can before we start making babies.

If you enjoy King's Promise, download Dmitry's story in Brutal Promise, available at my shopzoebethgeller online.

Want to read the next book before anyone else? Check out my pre-orders on my site.

ALSO BY ZOE BETH GELLER

Stop by shopzoebethgeller.com and get your pre-orders early. I offer bundle deals, audios, books in German and so much more!

Dirty: A Dark Mafia Romance Series

Micheli Mafia

Italian King: A Dark Mafia Romance Book 1

Dirty Vengeance: A Dark Mafia Romance Book 2

Dirty Bargain: A Dark Mafia Romance Book 3

Dirty Born: A Dark Mafia Romance Book 4

Dirty Deals: A Dark Mafia Romance Book 5

Volkov Bratva

King's Promise

Brutal Promise

Sinful Promise

Borrelli Mafia

Mafia King: Matteo

Zoe's Facebook fan group

ZBG Mafia Fan Group

Maine Megaladons Football Series

Faking it with the Football Star

The Player's Obsession

Scoring with the Coach's Daughter

Maine Maulers Hockey Series

Maine Maulers Hockey Series

Rookie in Love (now in audio)

Jagged Ice

Hotter than Puck

Benched by the Nanny

Puck in the Oven

Pucking the Team Captain

Pucking with the Goalie

Sin Bin Hockey Series

Tyler: Hooked (Free prequel to the series)

The Sin Bin Hockey Series

Jackson: Against the Boards

Alan: Between the Pipes

Erik: Fire and Ice

Blayze: Slap Shot

Paavo: The Defender

Spencer: Penalty Box

Isak: Coach

Kaden: Game Time

Liam: The Enforcer

Jake: Roughing

Facebook fan group for sports

Zoe Beth Geller's Hockey Pond Reader

I love espresso and escaping into the worlds I weave. I write the genres I love. I'm a compulsive overachiever and workaholic but I enjoy my fan groups as I get to know my readers and if you love my books, I hope to see you there! The life of an author is one that never sleeps so the groups provide a way for me to interact with you!

Want to sign up for the low down on my next work in progress? Would you like to be the first for a sneak peek at my chapters? Join my mafia newsletter Click Here

Want to be an ARC reader? Click here Choose hockey or mafia or both. It's like shopping, tons of options!

I love the reader (fan) groups! It's a place I drop in and get to know my readers and fans!

If mafia is your jam, sign up for my newsletter at **shopzoebethgeller.com**

Fan Groups
Zoe Beth Geller's Hockey Pond
ZBG Mafia Romances

Follow me on TT at zoebethgellerauthor1

www.ingramcontent.com/pod-product-compliance
Lightning Source LLC
Chambersburg PA
CBHW071435200726
48294CB00002B/650